Don't Skip "Breakfast"

Edgar Award Nominee for Best Mystery Novel of the Year and Best First Mystery from the Mystery Writers of America
and
Nominated for the Last Laugh Award from the Crime Writers Association, England

Breakfast With a Cereal Killer is a **refreshing, funny...well-written mystery**, with **DECEPTIVE CLUES**, *distinctive characters*, and imaginable settings.

Geoffrey Gamble is a delightful, creative, and **invigorating** new author, [and his book] will **grab** and keep your attention, leave you reading all night, then have you **looking forward to [his] next novel** at the breakfast table the following morning.

-- **Larry A. Bailey**
The Open Book, Sacramento, CA

Cute story, dahling. . . congratulations! I dash[ed] out this weekend and [found] myself a copy. . . then **I gagged on my Coco Puffs** trying to find out who was ruining Chestnut Grove's **most important meal of the day.**

-- **Farrow Stephenson, aka "Farrow the Fed-Ex Guy"**
KBGG 98.1 FM Radio, San Francisco

Be sure to check out **THE CEREAL KILLER WEB SITE** at:
http://members.aol.com/Exposethis/DecentExposure/books.html

Don't Skip "Breakfast"

From its punny title, to its copyright page (listing trademarks for 14 cereal brands), right through to its ending both ***logical*** and **daffy**, **Geoffrey P. Gamble's** mystery debut is **a blend of arch, witty writing** and amusingly off-kilter plotting set in a fictional San Francisco Bay Area small town.

Breakfast With a Cereal Killer is stuffed with comfortable genre stereotypes, including **a gruff cop**. . . **a hard-driving newspaper editor**, and an eager-to-advance openly GAY REPORTER -- and ***no shortage of murder victims,*** apparently offed by their Cocoa Puffs.

MYSTERY BUFFS will find *a queer twist* to their favored reading, and fans of the adroit quip will find *plenty to smile about.*

-- Richard Labonte
A Different Light, San Francisco

Breakfast with a Cereal Killer

Breakfast with a Cereal Killer

Book Orange in The Rainbow Mystery Series

Geoffrey P. Gamble

Geoffrey P. Gamble
2011

DECENT EXPOSURE PRESS

Washington D.C. • Oakland, California

Published by Decent Exposure Press
Washington, DC / Oakland, California

For information, inquiries, or order requests, contact:
Decent Exposure Press
PO Box 6612
Oakland, California 94603
e-mail address: Exposethis@aol.com
or visit our Web Site at
http://members.aol.com/Exposethis/DecentExposure/books.html

Limited Edition First Printing: April 1997
Second Printing: August 1997
10 9 8 7 6 5 4 3 2

Library of Congress Catalog Card Number: 96-93083
ISBN 0-9656044-0-3

Printed in the United States of America
Cover Production by Felix DeJesus
Cover Concept by Lardook

PUBLISHER'S NOTE

This is a work of fiction. Names, characters, places, and incidents are the products of the author's imagination or are used fictitiously. Any resemblance to actual persons, living or dead, events, or locales is entirely coincidental.

Literary references to certain breakfast cereal names, brands, products, or slogans are done in jest, without malicious intent or inference. (REMEMBER: Cereals don't kill people. People kill people.)

No breakfast food was harmed or mistreated in any way during the conception, writing, or printing of this novel.

To Sharyn McCrumb —

for showing me the ropes
and quietly making sure I didn't hang myself
with one of them

Breakfast with a Cereal Killer

Chapter One

The Breakfast of Champions

MATTHEW BLACK *HATED* MORNINGS, and anyone who knew him knew that.

For the better part of his thirty-three years, he fought an internal body clock that seemed to be set on some warped version of Daylight Savings Time, only in reverse.

At first, this was not a problem, for as an infant, he would easily sleep through the night and well into the next morning, much to his parent's surprise and delight. As he grew older, however, it became more of a nuisance as he tried to stay in bed until eleven each day, ignoring any pesky alarm clock buzzer, loud plea from his mother, or phone call from an irate employer. If he *did* manage to get up any earlier than ten-thirty, he would either lumber around like one of the living dead, or he'd grumble and bitch through a formidable scowl that would keep nearly everyone else at bay.

Nothing in life seemed important enough to call Matthew from his much-loved slumber. No school assignment. No television show. No young woman who fancied him. No job.

Nothing, that is, until he was introduced to the joy of running by his high school gym teacher, Mr. Eddleston, in the spring of his freshman year.

Matthew Black found that he had a gift in running, and by the end of his sophomore term, he had landed a starting position on the Varsity Track Team at Marshall Clancy High and was shattering any and all records at the school and throughout the San Francisco Bay area. Each day, he got up before the sun and could be found sprinting his way around his neighborhood or jogging around the school's paved lanes. At Eddleston's insistence, he signed up for the 1980 Olympic Team try-outs held during his senior year, and to no one's surprise but his own, he earned a spot on the American roster for the Summer Games.

For the small East Bay city of Chestnut Grove, California, it was a remarkable story of Local Boy making good. For young Matthew Black, it was an opportunity and the thrill of a lifetime.

Then, half a globe away, world events conspired to shatter his dreams forever. The Soviet Union invaded the small country of Afghanistan, and as a result, the United States boycotted the Games in Moscow. Matt's chance for the Gold disappeared, at least, for the next four years, then was lost entirely when he tore ligaments in his right knee during a tag football game with friends.

He had balked at college for the time being, choosing to sign a short list of contracts for product endorsements instead. He pushed running shoes and sweat pants, kid's toys and video games, shampoo and a spray for jock itch. He even ended up as the coverboy for the cereal touted as "the breakfast of champions."

When a cub reporter for the local newspaper caught wind that the town's celebrity didn't actually *like* Wheaties, however — or anything else associated with mornings for that matter — the *Times* ran a cover story on "the truth in advertising" that ended those dreams as well. The ensuing scandal forced Matthew Black out of the spotlight and back into his small house in Chestnut Grove. The endorsement deals dried up a few weeks later.

He spent the rest of his twenties dodging photographers who now only wanted a shot of the fallen hero. He even banned all cameras at his wedding held on his thirty-first birthday. That relationship lasted all of seven months.

Matthew Black didn't sit still for a camera again until February 19, 1993, but it wasn't as if he had any choice.

"Victim's house, interior, kitchen," came the voice of Chestnut Grove's police detective Hunter Whitloe. "Breakfast nook, left wall, kitchen table, body, taken from front door."

The flash from his assistant's Nikon went off, momentarily bleaching out the scene. "Got it," said Deputy Jonathan Briggs. "Exposure 27?"

Matthew Black sat hunched over his glass-topped kitchen table, arms out to his side, and face half-drowned in a large bowl of milk. He wore only a pair of gray sweat pants, and milk drenched the exposed upper portion of his chest. Much of it had pooled in his crotch. His left eye and the half of his mouth not in the bowl were open, surrounded by Wheaties, which were everywhere.

"Looks like he choked on the stuff," Briggs noted, indicating the overturned box of cereal next to the dead man's head. He readied himself for his partner's next set of instructions to frame another picture.

"I don't think so," Whitloe said simply.

He knew the deceased, Matthew Black, or *knew of him*, anyway. His being found like this, at 8:27 in the morning no less, was no accident. Ironic, perhaps; a little funny, maybe; but certainly no accident.

"What then?" the deputy asked, lowering his camera. "Hey, maybe it's a suicide."

The detective had worked with the young officer long enough to know that he wasn't kidding. "Shut up, Briggs," he said, controlling his temper. "Just shut up." He took a few steps over to the body as the coroner's car and an ambulance pulled up in front of the house. "Okay. Back to work. Exposure 27. . ."

***

"Hey, Blazer. Can I see you for a minute?"

I looked up from my small desk in the *Times* newsroom just as Assistant News Editor Charlotte Journigan, my boss, slipped behind the door to her office. Actually, I was so low on the pecking order of the staff of the local newspaper, that nearly *everyone* here was my boss; Charlotte just happened to be the highest ranking person in the office at that moment. "I'll be right there," I called after her, reaching for a pad of paper and a pen.

"Paul, could you get me a refill on your way back?"

It was Otto Nicholson, another one of my bosses. Nicholson penned the paper's obituaries, and my present assignment was working under him, doing background searches and fact verification whenever necessary.

"Sure thing," I said. I took his coffee mug from his wizened hand as I passed by.

I had been on the staff of the *Times* for five months now, since last October when I decided to shelve my chosen career as an English teacher for something that would bring in a little more money. Substituting in the high schools in and around Chestnut Grove while waiting for a more permanent position didn't actually guarantee a steady income, and landing that occasional teaching job had become far more difficult after the fact that I was gay came out during the publicity of a little trial where I was up for murder.

But that's another story, and now nearly a year and a half later, it seemed like ancient history.

(Let's just say that I *didn't* kill her, and the person who did got off with a suspended sentence when they were looking to give me life.

If I sound bitter, maybe it's because I am. I didn't appreciate spending six months of my life in jail awaiting trial for a crime I didn't commit; and the details of my personal life — and those of one of my friend's — didn't have to go public in the way they did, just because a bigoted police department, and one detective in particular, liked to rake mud and call it an investigation.

I did learn something from the whole experience though. Living in the closet in a town like Chestnut Grove could be deadly in and of itself. I had to be "out," not only for me being true to myself, but to take away the possibility of my sexuality being used against me from anyone who might choose to do so. Everyone here on the newspaper staff knew I was gay, and in fact, I only took the job when I read in my contract that they could not discriminate "on the basis of sexual orientation.")

"Blazer, are you coming?" the news editor said loudly. "I haven't got all . . ."

"Day," I said, finishing her sentence as I slipped through her office door and took a seat in front of her. "Sorry. Right here, Chief. What is it?"

"Don't call me 'Chief,'" Charlotte Journigan said. Her voice had a drawl as thick as Carolina tree sap, and having spent most of my life in Virginia, it kind of reminded me of home. These days, that wasn't such a bad thing.

"Sorry. . .Ms. Journigan."

"Charlotte's fine. You've been with us long enough. You can drop the formalities. Besides, you've seen me on deadline."

I laughed. All of that good southern upbringing went right out the window when Charlotte Journigan saw a deadline approaching. She could swear a blue streak, combining as many as nine expletives together in a single sentence that would just make you stop and listen in amazement. I once overheard her, in one of her fits, refer to herself as "This castrating, sorry-assed father-fucking bitch." I wondered if "Ms. Bitch" would have been too informal at this moment, however, I suspected that we'd both get a good laugh out of it. "Charlotte," I said simply.

"Paul, I've heard from someone on the News desk that one of our local celebrities died this morning, and I'd like you to do a special side bar on him."

"'Local celebrities'?" I repeated. "I didn't know we had any. Besides, Nicholson does the obits. I just do the digging."

"Nice pun," Charlotte said. She lit a cigarette and took a deep drag. "Otto will still do the standard notice." She exhaled a long stream of smoke. "We just need to do an extended piece on this one, and I think you're able enough to handle it."

I smiled a little at her remark, knowing that this woman was not all too free with her compliments, and that this was as close to one as I could expect. "Just who was this guy anyway?" I asked.

"Chestnut Grove's Olympic hopeful Matthew Black," she replied. "You'll find out all you need to know about him in the morgue."

Chapter Two

Un-lucky Charms

"FIND ANYTHING INTERESTING?" ASKED Otto Nicholson, stepping into the newspaper's archive room, also known as "the morgue," and closing the door behind him.

"Just the usual, so far," I replied. I sat behind an ancient microfilm viewer, and old issues of the *Times* scrawled by on the illuminated screen before me. "It seems pretty sad, really. All of that hard work and effort trashed because of events completely beyond your control. I was still in high school when we boycotted the Olympics, and. . ."

"Oh, that's not the half of it," Otto interrupted. "That's right," he continued as he took a seat next to me and searched through a stack of other microfilm reels, "you weren't around here then."

Pulling a reel dated October through December 1980, he rethreaded the machine, and I watched as more pages of history flashed by. "There," he said, pointing. "What do you think of that?"

The article read: "BLACK-ENED IMAGE — The Truth About Our Athlete and The Products He Endorses," and the accompanying copy tore through both the credibility of Chestnut Grove's Olympic track star and the notoriety he had hoped to glean from backing everything from sweatsuits to cereal.

"Youch," I said as I read the piece. "But what was the big deal? A lot of people don't use the things they push. It's all an advertising gimmick."

"Not in the seventies and early eighties," Otto corrected. "This was all still very post-Watergate, and ever since Woodward and Bernstein, the press had a new-found sense of watchdogging the world. The Truth had to be exposed, no matter what the cost. The public had a right to know."

I looked from Nicholson back to the article on the screen. Pushing the PRINT button at the corner of the viewer, the machine made a whirring sound, went dark for a moment, then spit out a paper copy on the side. The lighted image returned as I picked up the hardcopy sheet. "I'm all for freedom of speech and freedom of the press, Otto, but something like this cost ol' Matthew Black here his life, his career. I don't think that's entirely fair."

"You've got a lot to learn about this business, my friend," Nicholson said with a slight laugh. "Look at it this way. This story wasn't completely destructive. It helped launch the career of one of the best newspapermen this area's ever known." Gesturing to the page I held in front of me, he guided my attention to the article's by-line.

Garrison Fitzgerald.

The man was to the *Times* something like what Rupert Murdoch had been to the *New York Post*.

Otto had fed me a few stories about the man over the past few months. It seems that the *Times* had been given to young Fitzgerald by his wealthy parents at the tune of $20 million as a present for his graduation from journalism school at the local community college in 1978. He saw the *Times* as a newspaper in need of direction, in need of new blood, in need of a change, and he saw himself as the man to do it.

Competing with the Hearst-owned giants of the *San Francisco Chronicle* and *Examiner* had nearly driven the paper under, and Fitzgerald — on a whim or, as Otto recalled, a dare — sought to change its image from a rather dull and predictable imitation, to a flashy, interesting trendsetter. Under his direction, the paper continued to feature crime, scandal and gossip, along with the standard Murdoch-copied circulation builders like contests and serialized features. He also fought to expand the paper's news coverage, to strengthen the sports and business sections, and to add greater local entertainment and arts coverage.

The greatest change came, however, when he publicly threw off the reins of his position and picked up a pencil and tape recorder to become another one of the paper's reporters in early 1980.

"They laughed at him, at first, you know," Nicholson recalled, "but when he started putting out pieces like this, just about everyone took pause." He thought for a moment, remembering. "The kid was brilliant, and he sure gave the seasoned folk like me a run. He could crank out an expose like this one just as easily as he could write hard news, a sports editorial, or advertising copy, for that matter. If you were stuck working on something, go to Garry. He'd always have the best answer, the one that would get the job done for you."

"Where's Fitzgerald now?" I asked, noting that my own position on staff had, in part, come about after the prominent newspaperman had left the *Times* nearly half a year ago, with little fanfare or explanation. Five or so others had been hired to fill in, but somehow much of the gap he left still remained. I felt it most whenever I talked with one of the senior staff members, like Nicholson.

"Indefinite leave," he replied. "After a significant family tragedy, he decided to take some time off to reassess his priorities. He'd become rather disenchanted with life here at the *Times*, and when his wife and little girl were killed in a car accident, he saw little reason to stay on."

"That's terrible."

"Well," Otto said, "knowing Garry as I did, I bet he's taken this time to plot out his next great adventure, probably as far away from publishing as he can get."

"Well," I said, "*my* next adventure should be getting this sidebar done for the afternoon edition. I wouldn't want to find myself on Charlotte's bad side."

"I don't blame you," he agreed, getting up. "Let me know if there's anything else I can help you with."

"Thanks, I'll do that." I paused a bit as he made it toward the door. "We're still on at lunch, aren't we?" When I had seen him jogging each day at noon at the start of the month, I had asked if he wouldn't mind some company. By now it had become a ritual of sorts, and we kept each other motivated.

"Wouldn't miss it," he said. "You may want to wear an extra shirt or something today. I noticed it was rather chilly this morning on the way in."

"Sure thing," I said, almost hearing my dad in what he said. I warmed a little. "Meet you at the elevators," I managed to get out as the morgue's door closed behind him.

***

As the morgue's door opened, Chestnut Grove's deputy coroner Tess Taggert looked up from the remains of the elderly woman who lay on the steel slab in front of her. "Malone, thank God," she said to her bald partner, the city's Number Two medical examiner, as he entered the cool, white-tiled room. "I've got another one here, and I just can't. . ."

Redford Malone strode over to where Taggert stood and bent toward the head of the deceased. As he had done countless times before, he brought his hands to the dead woman's head and with steady fingers deftly removed the pierced earrings she wore, first the left lobe, then the right. Straightening up, he gave them to his partner, gingerly cupping her outstretched hand in his own for effect.

"I swear, Toe Tag," he said, using one of her nicknames, "you can Y-cut these stiffs from tits to toes like you're carving up Thanksgiving turkey, but I still can't for the life of me get what your problem is with removing a dead woman's earrings."

"Don't give me any lip, cue-ball," she replied, trying to cover her embarrassment with an acid tongue. "Just be sure you don't stray too far. I think I've got a couple others with them, too."

"Anything for you, doll, but I don't think Miss Kravitz's acute angina is going to stay on the front burner for long after you see what I've just dragged in with me."

"I wouldn't be slicing her, Malone, if this were just angina," Taggert spat, half-listening. "I think she doubled up on her medication in order to end it all, and. . ."

"Hey, Doc," Hunter Whitloe said simply as he entered. Trailing him were a black body bag on a gurney and his assistant, Jonathan Briggs. "Can I see you over here?" He allowed Briggs to wheel by and meet Redford Malone at the other end of the room.

"What'd ya got there, Hunter?" she asked, approaching him. "Belated Valentine's Day present? I never knew you cared."

Whitloe shot her a look that said he wasn't in the mood. "It's Matthew Black," he said in a grave tone. "We found him this morning, face-first in a bowl of Wheaties."

Tess Taggert tried to stifle a laugh. "*'Wheaties'?* If I remember correctly, he wouldn't be caught dead near the stuff." Black's rise and fall replayed itself in her mind.

"Well," Whitloe replied, "that seems to be just what happened. That's what's got me worried."

Taggert turned to watch Malone and Briggs remove the body from the bag and onto an examination table. As she and Whitloe approached, she could make out a dried wheat flake or two on the deceased's shoulder and what appeared to be a half-chewed mouthful just inside his lips. Raising a hand to dismiss them so her work could begin, she said, "I'll let you know what I find."

***

"I like it," Charlotte Journigan said to me as she returned my sidebar on Matthew Black.

The smile I had weakened a little as I flipped through the four type-written pages I'd submitted. A quick glance showed that she must have sliced open an artery and bled all over it. I couldn't find a single sentence that had made it past her unscathed.

"Nice style, Paul," she reaffirmed through an exhale of cigarette smoke. "Very well thought out. Good structure and flow. You'll note that I did clean it up a little, though. I pulled out all that stuff about his Fall From Grace. No real need for it here." She extinguished her Camel by dropping it into a small Taco Bell cup with an inch of water in it. It gave a quick hiss and a final wisp of smoke before dying and floating among the other butts.

"But I thought it was important," I managed to say. "It was news, and. . ."

"*'Was'* is the operative word here, Blazer. Hardly something I'd like to have dredged up about me when I bite it, and I think in this instance, the late Mr. Black just might agree with me."

As she lit another Camel, Otto Nicholson knocked lightly on her door and poked his head in. "If Paul's piece is ready, I can run it over to typesetting with my obit," he offered. He came in carrying his own page of copy and a new Taco Bell cup in his free hand. "And I can take that, too, if you want," he said, indicating Charlotte Journigan's makeshift ashtray.

"Good man, Nicholson," she said, and she handed him her dirty cup for the new one. An instant later, she flicked a hunk of ash from her cigarette into the clean water. Looking back at me, she asked, "So, do you agree with me? It is *your* by-line, after all."

I only gave a thin smile and a slight nod, and I handed my piece to Otto.

"Fine," Charlotte said. "Now stick around for a minute or two, and I'll find something else for you to work on."

I pulled out my notepad and pen, then eased back in my chair as Otto Nicholson left, armed with my bloodied copy, his obituary, and a cup half-filled with stagnant cigarette water.

Although it was only about forty degrees outside, I could feel the sweat begin to collect in the crooks of my elbows, the small of my back, and at the base of my neck as Otto and I rounded into the third mile of our lunch-hour run. I had measured our stretch once with a ride in my Jeep, and it clocked in at 4.2 miles. Some days, it took all I had to get it done before we had to be back in the office, but today I was making really good time. I always seemed to run better when I had something on my mind, as if I were trying to run away from it, or something.

"What's bothering you, Paul?" Nicholson said, noticing.

"Nothing," I said automatically. After a few more paces, however, I conceded. "It's just. . ." I started between measured breaths, "I can't seem. . .to get anything past her. . .without her ripping it. . .apart."

We strode on a few more paces before he replied.

"I wouldn't worry about it too much, Paul," he said evenly. "Charlotte likes you. She likes what you do."

"Sometimes. . .I get the feeling. . .that she just hacks it up to put. . .her mark on it," I panted. "She's just. . .got to change it because. . .she didn't write it."

"Maybe," Otto replied. "But I doubt it. She wouldn't give you an assignment if she didn't think you could handle it."

If I weren't so winded I might have laughed at this second-hand compliment. The best I could afford was a thin smile as I looked over at him. "Thanks," I said. "I needed that."

"Couldn't tell," he said sarcastically.

My smile broadened until I realized that he was stepping up the pace for the last mile. With some effort, I moved to keep up with him.

"That's better," he said. "You were beginning to lag behind a bit."

Turning my head to the side, I hacked a wad of spit into the passing grass. "Right," I replied. "Just don't let me pass you. . .old man."

Otto gave a hearty laugh as he kicked it into gear I had no hope of matching. I continued on at my top speed as he easily surged ahead and disappeared into the distance.

I caught up with him again in the basement-level locker room of the *Times* building. There wasn't much to it — a couple of lockers, a treadmill that was "Under Repair" more than half the time, a stationary bicycle, half a set of free weights — but it gave us a place to change clothes, towel off, and shower if we had time. Otto was midway through his post-run stretches when I plopped on the bench beside him.

"You're amazing," I said, out of breath. Reaching down, I took off my right shoe.

"The key, my friend, is a good breakfast. Be sure to eat your Wheaties."

"Unless you're Matthew Black," I quipped.

Otto offered a dry laugh before stripping down and heading for the shower. "Yeah, see where that got him."

I loosened the laces on my left shoe and took it off, smiling ear to ear. Finally, someone else who sometimes side-stepped the tasteful or politically correct for a good laugh every now and again. I knew I liked this guy for a reason, I thought, and I pulled my sweatshirt over my head.

***

Tess Taggert and Redford Malone had spent the better part of the morning weighing, measuring, and x-raying the corpse of Matthew Black. Deputy Briggs remained long enough to fire off a round of photographs of the body, both clothed, and later, nude. He left around ten with half a dozen rolls of film, Black's pair of dull gray sweatpants appropriately bagged and marked with an evidence tag, a full set of the victim's fingerprints, and what appeared to be a pair of latents lifted from the underside of his neck. These would later be joined by the usual array of fluid, fiber, and tissue samples taken to the experts at the Criminalistics Laboratory Division of the Contra Costa sheriff's department, located in the nearby town of Martinez.

"Toxicology should report back within a week," Taggert said aloud, but to no one in particular. In fact, the only other sets of ears in the exam room now were Malone's and the non-working pair belonging to the deceased on the table in front of her. She secretly thought though — no, *hoped* was a better word — that hearing herself think aloud might have her see what she felt she was missing. "But I don't know what more they'll be able to tell us.

"He's got all the classic signs of a cafe coronary: bits of food lodged firmly in the throat, preventing any kind of breathing, talking, or screaming; fingerprints on his neck as a sign he reached there in a state of panic as he lost air; and petechiae in the conjunctiva, caused by increased pressure in the head during the event. Hell, he even has milk residue up his nose and a slight swelling of the tongue, all of which all point back to that murderous bowl of corn flakes."

"I thought it was *Wheaties*, Toe," Malone interjected.

"That's the part that gets me," she replied. "That, and this little mark over here." She pointed to a slightly reddish welt, about an inch long, on Matthew Black's chest, some three inches below his left nipple.

"Scar?" Malone offered. "Burn mark, perhaps."

Taggert moved closer to the body and examined the small swelling for the umpteenth time. "I considered all that," she said, sounding exasperated, "but I don't think so." She straightened up and crossed her arms at her chest. "Beats the hell out of me."

"What do you think old Hunter'll say when you tell him the guy just bit off more that he could chew, literally?"

"Don't take me there, Malone. I don't even want to think about it."

Murder investigations weren't a common thing in Chestnut Grove, and Lieutenant Detective Hunter Whitloe wondered long and hard if he really were looking at the start of one with the Matthew Black case.

Most of the violent crime that happened on the east side of the San Francisco Bay seemed limited to the neighboring cities of Oakland, Richmond, or Vallejo. On occasion, you'd hear of something happening in the more upscale areas of Walnut Creek, Pleasant Hill, or Alamo, but for the most part, Whitloe's jurisdiction reported only the minor things. Convenience store robberies happened, but not to an alarming degree. Drug deals, quite thankfully, managed to keep to a two-block section on the industrial side of town, making them easy to watch and control. And the only reported rape in recent memory turned out to be a scorned housewife crying "wolf" in an effort to get her cheating husband in more trouble than he was in already.

Since his promotion to Special Investigations in August of 1990, Whitloe had been in on the business end of only two murders in Chestnut Grove. The last had occurred over a Christmas turkey and had a bevy of witnesses who were home for the holiday, so there hadn't been much call for a real criminal investigation. The first, a restaurant hostess bludgeoned to death with a piece of office equipment, Whitloe classified as "problematic," with all the right evidence pointing to the wrong suspect. And having that joker Jonathan Briggs assigned to assist didn't help matters much either.

That case, now nearly a year and a half ago, had the detective consider all the facts before plunging headlong into calling this morning's scene a "murder."

Whitloe had questioned the kid who had discovered the body — the morning newspaper boy out on his before-school rounds, late as usual — and came up with little out of the ordinary. The kid had been instructed by the victim in a note taped to the porch on the previous morning to be sure to stop by to discuss the service he'd been getting lately. And, yes, the boy was able to provide said note when asked.

Seeing the main door of the house open when he arrived, he ventured inside, calling Mr. Black's name. He stopped when he saw the deceased hunched over his breakfast and bolted to the nearest pay phone to call 911. Morbid curiosity and the almost-sure excuse from the police that would clear any tardiness at school had the boy stay until Whitloe arrived on the scene. When questioned, he knew little else.

There appeared to be no forced entry, no sign of struggle or fight, no excessive marks on the body.

Just the cereal.

That fucking cereal, thought Hunter Whitloe. He pounded a fist on the top of his desk.

That was the only thing about it all that didn't sit right.

Wouldn't it be funny, though, if on the day Matthew Black finally made peace with one of the things that led to his downfall, it somehow rose up and snuffed him, out of pure spite? Whitloe imagined a confident Matthew Black buying a box of Wheaties at the local Save Mart, taking it home with a gallon of 2% milk, and thinking himself on top of the world as he sat down in front of a cereal bowl with an extra large spoon.

Then he saw the town's Olympic hopeful swell up and gag as he forced a mouthful of the wheat flakes into his lips. With eyes bulging and his face turning three shades of blue, he drops face-first into his old nemesis, to have any last breath drown itself out in the milk.

Whitloe could almost see the three cartoon figures of Snap, Crackle, and Pop doing some bizarre dance of death around the kitchen table as Matthew Black breathed his last.

Okay, he conceded, *wrong cereal,* but he had to admit, it was kind of funny. Hey, maybe Tony the Tiger came in to announce, "They're GRRREAT!" and he left the door open on his way out.

Then it hit him.

"Shit," he said aloud as he picked up the phone and dialed.

"Coroner's office," came a voice on the other end.

"Hunter Whitloe here. Chestnut Grove P.D. Let me talk to Taggert."

There was a pause. "Dr. Taggert can't come to the phone right now. May I take a message?"

"Poison," Whitloe blurted. "Tell her to be sure to test the cereal for some type of poison. The milk, too, for that matter."

"Pardon?"

The detective sighed, wondering if he really sounded as crazy as he thought he must have just then. "For the case I brought in to her this morning. Ask her to check for. . ."

"'Poison,'" the voice filled in.

"Yeah," Whitloe said. "In what he ate."

"'The cereal.'"

"Yes, the cereal."

"And 'the milk, too.'"

He fumed. "Just be sure she gets the message, okay?" He slammed down the receiver before he could get a response. A beat later, he smiled. He *knew* there was going to be much more to this.

***

"Hey, Paul. Let's call it a day. You want a ride home?"

"Sure, Otto. Thanks," I said, straightening up my desk as I got up. "Just let me drop this draft on Charlotte's desk on the way out."

"Another assignment? See, I told you she likes you. You're well on your way around here."

"Maybe I'll be the next Garrison Fitzgerald," I said with a laugh as I came out of the Assistant News Editor's office. I got a stern look from Otto that had me pause.

"I don't think so, Blazer," he said. "There'll only be *one* Garrison Fitzgerald. I don't care how good she thinks you are or how good *you* think you are, you aren't about to replace him."

I followed him cautiously. "Otto, I'm sorry. I didn't mean anything by it. I hope you're not upset that I. . ."

Nicholson turned abruptly with a softened smile on his face. "Paul, forgive me. I was out of line. I shouldn't have bitten your head off like that."

"You two were close," I ventured.

"Professionally, yes," he replied. "It was good to have him around. He kept me on my toes, always trying to do a better job."

"And you miss him," I added.

"Of course I miss him," he said with a little of the sharpness from before. "We *all* do." He paused and took a deep breath. "It's not as if we were best friends, or anything. We didn't spend time together outside this place, but I. . ."

"I understand," I interrupted, trying to shift the topic to something more comfortable. "Do you mind if we stop at the pet store on the way home? I need to pick up some dog food."

"I didn't know you had a dog," he said, much lighter.

"Yeah, a Doberman. A friend gave him to me about a year and a half ago. I guess he's about five now."

"'A Doberman,'" Otto repeated. "Mean?"

"Nah. He's just a big baby."

"What's his name?"

"Dante," I said. "From *Dante's Inferno*, I think. Dominic thought he was the hound from hell when it came to paper training him."

"'Dominic?'" Otto asked.

I smiled. "Nothing gets past you, does it?"

"You two were close," he said, parroting me earlier. "And you miss him."

"That was a long time ago," I said, more for my own benefit than his. "We got along in a very basic way, at gut-level, but just wasn't the right time for anything long-term, I guess."

"Well, you got the dog. *That's* long-term."

With a chuckle, I agreed, "Yeah."

"He'll be back," Otto guessed. "Some day."

As we walked by the circulation desk, I found myself happy that I could talk to someone about that part of my life without feeling judged or having to apologize or explain. With Otto, my being gay seemed to be as important or as significant as my having green eyes, or a mustache. "Someday," I said, "when you have time, I'll tell you the whole story."

He gave a brief nod, and we passed the Complaint Desk to overhear the fair-haired Pollyanna assigned to the job — twenty-year-old Cindi Bates — say into the phone: "Pardon me, sir. What was that? . . . No, the part *before* 'you stupid, fucking asshole.'"

I looked over to see she was completely unfazed by the abuse she was getting, *and* she was writing down *everything* the person was saying.

"Now is 'brain dead' one word, or two. . ."

Otto opened the door to the outside. "Another satisfied customer."

"Thanks, Joe," Nicholson said, taking a set of car keys from a man in a *Times* T-shirt on the loading dock. "I'll take good care of her."

"Do me a favor and drop off two bundles at the 7-Eleven on your way, will ya?" asked Joe.

"Sure. No problem," Otto said.

We walked into the parking lot, and Otto slid a key into the driver's door of one of the newspaper delivery vans lined alongside the building. He threw a *Times* apron over his shoulders as he climbed in and unlocked the passenger side for me.

"Gotta wear one of these when I drive this thing," he explained.

"What happened to your car?" I asked, recalling the VW bug I had seen him in a few months earlier.

"I had to put it in the shop. Gear trouble. I think it's just the clutch, but I'm sure the damned mechanic will try to convince me to replace the whole transmission again." He turned the ignition key and fired up the engine. It rumbled like an old school bus.

"Nice of them to let you use this," I said.

"Work here long enough, Blazer, and you'll find that a few people owe you a favor or two." With that, he thrust the long stick shift into reverse, backed us out of the lot, and started us on the way.

After stopping at the 7-Eleven to deliver the afternoon edition of the *Times*, as promised, we drove to Chestnut Grove's PetCo. On the way, I browsed through the paper to find my article, next to Nicholson's obituary.

"What a way to go," Otto said, glancing my way.

"Yeah," I said. "Choking to death on your least favorite cereal." I flipped to the news report titled, "FORMER OLYMPIC HOPEFUL FOUND DEAD AT HOME," and scanned it. "It seems a little strange, don't you think?"

"If you ask me, I think it's kind of funny. Like karma, or something. He probably deserved it."

With a sharp bump, the van pulled into the PetCo parking lot.

"Sorry about that," Otto said. "I guess this thing could use a new set of shocks." He jumped out the driver's door when we stopped and called to me, "Come on."

I hoisted a 40-pound bag of dog food on the counter and began to reach for my wallet when Otto rounded an aisle and asked, "Do you think that'll be enough?"

"It usually gets me through three weeks or so. Got to keep him well fed. I'm not sure I want 90 pounds of angry Doberman greeting me when I get home."

"I see your point. I. . ."

"Mr. Nicholson," interrupted the store manager, calling from the fish and aquarium supply department. "Have you seen our new shipment of marine fish?"

Otto walked his way, and I nodded to the pock-marked boy behind the counter, "I'll be right back."

"How long have you had them?" Otto was asking as I entered the semi-dark tank room. He and the store manager stood before a 125-gallon display with what I recognized as black volitaire lionfish.

"Since last Thursday," the manager replied. "We lost one in the move, but the rest are quite healthy, I assure you."

"Beautiful lionfish," I said. "I've never been able to keep a salt-water tank myself."

"*Scorpaena guttata,*" Otto corrected me. "A black scorpionfish, to be more accurate, Paul. These are from the Indo-Pacific," he said with a glance to the manager.

"Quite right," he confirmed. "And they have been net-caught, not gassed."

"Gassed?" I asked.

"Some of the less-reputable dealers obtain their fish from catchers who use some type of gas to stun the fish so they are easily retrieved," Otto explained.

"We find that many of those do not survive the trip to the States," the store manager chimed in, "and most of those that do have been damaged in the catching process."

"That," Otto continued, "or it's all far too stressful." He looked back at the tank, raising a hand to the glass. Instinctively, the scorpionfish nearest him erected its row of poisonous dorsal spines and fanned out its fins in an impressive display. "Since last Thursday, you said?"

"And they all have a very healthy appetite. Four goldfish a day, each."

"Netted at some great depth, I'm sure," Otto said.

Although the size of the fish sometimes determined the price you'd find it for in the pet store, the depth at which it was caught was often more of a deciding factor in its final cost, I knew. The deeper the diver had to venture to get it, the higher the price. And, I assumed, being net-caught versus gassed would only help inflate the already high price.

"Not too deep," was the response, "but in treacherous reef waters, I'm afraid."

Nicholson sighed. "I'll take this one," he said, pointing.

"Very good, sir. And for you, such a frequent customer, a very special price." He looked around for a net and a double-lined plastic bag to snag Otto's fish. "By the way," he added as he opened the tank lid, "your other special order should arrive within the week."

Otto nodded. "Meet us at the counter. And I'll need a week's supply of feeders."

"Of course, sir. Right away."

"'Other special order'?" I asked, paying for my dog food.

"An octopus, from the Hawaiian Islands." The pock-marked kid rang up the scorpionfish and feeder goldfish at $160.00, plus tax.

"I'd like to see your tank some time," I said as we made our way to the *Times* van.

"Certainly, Paul. I'll have you over for dinner one evening."

"That'd be nice. Let me know when you're free."

The van rumbled in front of the house where I rented an attached in-law apartment.

"Want to meet my dog?" I asked.

"Sure. He won't bite me, will he?"

"I told you, he's harmless." I opened the door, turned on the light, and reached out a hand so that Dante could sniff me. With Otto right behind me carrying the dog food bag, I made the appropriate introductions. "Dante, this is my friend, Otto. Otto, Dante."

Setting down the bag, Otto tried, "Sit, boy."

But Dante didn't sit.

"You know," I explained, "that's one command he's never really learned. He'll do 'lay down,' 'roll over,' 'fetch,' and 'play dead,' but he never mastered 'sit.'" I looked at the dog. "It has me a little annoyed."

"Sit, Dante," Otto tried again, pushing on his hind quarters with his right hand as he spoke to him. "Sit."

The dog stood there, legs rigid, quietly refusing.

"Sit," he said again.

No response.

Just then, Otto sneezed. Twice.

"Gesundheit," I said.

And Dante sat down.

"Did you see that?" I asked.

"What would have him do that?

I decided to try it again. Lifting Dante to a standing position, I again said, "Gesundheit."

Dante sat once more.

"That's weird," Otto said.

Then I started laughing as it came to me. "No, that's *Dominic.*"

"Your friend? The one who gave him to you?"

I nodded. "Dante is half German shepherd, and it wouldn't surprise me if Dominic taught the dog some of his commands in German."

"But 'Gesundheit' doesn't mean 'sit.'"

"I know, but that's not the point. You can get a dog to sit by saying 'coffee' or to attack if you say 'O.J. Simpson' if you train them that way. It's all conditioned response." I looked down at the Doberman with wonder. "Just what do you have locked up there in that head of yours, *mein Hund*?"

Otto sneezed again, and said, "I may be allergic to him."

"Maybe you should go. I'll see you tomorrow."

"Good idea," he replied as he broke into a sneezing fit and left.

"Gesundheit," I repeated. Again the dog sat down.

I laughed until my sides hurt.

Chapter Three

Just Follow Your Nose

HUNTER WHITLOE'S WIFE, GLADYS, shuffled around their kitchen in the pre-dawn hours of Tuesday morning in her off-white terry cloth robe and an old pair of fuzzy, blue slippers. She couldn't sleep. Actually, it was Hunter who wouldn't *let* her sleep, with all that tossing and turning he had been doing lately.

She knew something at work had to be nagging at him. He never could rest well when there was. And his nights seemed to be more fitful ever since they found that former athlete dead four days ago.

But over the years, she had learned not to ask too much about police work. "Bore and gore," he would say. "Bore and gore."

Looking at his .357 Magnum hanging in its shoulder holster across a nearby chair, she figured he would end up firing off a few rounds at the shooting range in order to vent. He had always been proud of the fact that he had never had cause to fire it in the line of duty — he reminded her of that often — and there had been something to discharging it in a controlled environment that somehow calmed him.

Maybe he'd talk with some of the men on the force, but she doubted it. Hunter was more apt to stay quiet and stew than to share what he was thinking. He also had received a pretty good ribbing from some of his co-workers when he casually suggested turning in his weapon for a larger caliber, say a .41 or .44, although he knew the department wouldn't allow it. "Why get something bigger when you don't even use the one you have?" a few of the younger, more trigger-happy officers had said.

And although Hunter had told her about that conversation after she pressed rather hard, Gladys knew he would probably not open up to her right now. It was too soon.

As she turned on the TV, she silently decided that it was for the best. At least he didn't lie to her. He'd get that funny, tell-tale red wrinkle in the center of his chin when he did anyway, and she could see that a mile away.

Flipping to "Total Fitness," the morning cable-access exercise program, she decided she could continue to suffer him through times likes this, even if it meant that she lost a little sleep in the process.

"PLEASE STAND BY — WE'RE EXPERIENCING TECHNICAL DIFFICULTIES," read the hand-held placard on Channel 57 before her.

"That's odd," Gladys Whitloe mumbled to herself, expecting to see the familiar face of local fitness guru Terry Totah. She liked watching Terry. He was much closer to her own age than any of those leotard-wearing bimbos on the other channels, and he could stand to lose some weight himself. He was "real people," she would say, and sometimes, when she wasn't careful, she would find herself moving along with him and his half dozen or so equally out-of-shape fitness partners in the background.

Turning up the volume, she tried to make out some of the voices that mumbled in the background of the amateurishly produced show.

". . .seven-o-eight. . .and we're supposed to be on. . ." came one voice, very angry.

". . .the hell is he. . ." whispered another.

"You're up rather early, hon," said Hunter Whitloe as he entered from the bedroom, wearing only his pajama bottoms.

"Shhh," Gladys replied, a little startled. She pointed to the television without another word.

On screen, the "PLEASE STAND BY" placard came down to show one seriously overweight member of Terry Totah's exercise troupe move to the fore and improvise the start of the show.

"Good morning, Chestnut Grove," she said, trying to sound as relaxed as possible. "Let's move right on into our pre-workout stretches." With some effort, Terry's last-minute replacement moved her sizable girth into a toe-touching position. She reached just below her knees.

"Where's Terry Totah of '*Totah* Fitness'?" asked Hunter, mimicking the slight speech impediment that prevented Terry from saying his L's. Hunter thought it was kind of funny; Gladys found it endearing — more of his "real people" quality.

"I guess he's running a little late this morning," Gladys offered.

"That's public access TV for you," he replied. "They should take that shit off the air." He moved over to the refrigerator and opened it. "What's for breakfast?"

Since she found herself a little upset with his verbal bashing of Terry Totah, Gladys ignored Hunter's question for the moment. "Sleep well?" she asked instead.

"Not really," he said. "Bore and gore."

The phone rang.

"Hello," Gladys said, answering it. "Just a minute." Holding the receiver his direction, she said, "It's the station for you, Hunter."

He quickly swallowed the bite of apple he had managed to get in his mouth and lay the fruit on the counter. "Whitloe here."

Gladys watched as his expression changed. "Gore," she thought.

"When?" Hunter asked. "Who found him? Uh-huh. Have him stay there. Briggs? What does he. . .? No. If you can't find him, send Samuels instead. I'll be right there," he said, writing something down. "And don't touch anything until I get there. Yeah, bye."

Leaning over, he gave his wife a peck on the cheek before returning to the bedroom to change. "I'll eat later," he said. Within a few minutes, he came out, tucking a shirt into his pants. "Bet on a mid-season replacement," he said cryptically, pointing to the television. A moment later, he was gone.

Crunch. Crunch, crunch. Crunch.

Some joker's getting a good laugh out of this, Whitloe thought. His next step mashed even more of the cereal into the fibers of the carpet at the late Terry Totah's condo.

This time it was Total, and the former fitness fanatic sat in an easy chair in his living room, head back, gagged with a mouthful of it. Beside him was a collapsible TV tray with a half-empty cereal bowl, a glass of orange juice, and a plate with two slices of toast on it. Across a sea of flake-covered carpet, the television blared, playing his own exercise show.

"Turn that shit off," Hunter said, unable to hear himself think.

"But we haven't dusted for prints yet, Lieutenant," cautioned Samuels, the deputy on the scene.

"Goddamnit," Whitloe cursed. In the moment, though, he relaxed, realizing that had Deputy Jonathan Briggs been here, he probably would have marched right over and smeared any evidence by following through with the detective's order and turning off the set. He drew in a breath, then crunched his way behind the black lacquered entertainment center and yanked the power cord from the wall. The screen went blank. "That's better," he said, letting the cable drop.

Crunch.

"What's with all the cereal?" Samuels asked, surveying the scene.

Again, Whitloe thought of Briggs. *Suicide*, he'd say. "Some asshole's twisted sense of humor, I'm afraid."

"A '*cereal* killer,' Lieutenant?"

"Hmmph," was all Whitloe allowed as a reply. He looked over to Shannon McMillan, the film-school dropout and producer of "Total Fitness with Terry Totah," who had stormed over to the condo to roust his star and, in that process, had discovered the body. McMillan paced the small kitchenette from one end to the other, glancing toward them and biting his thumbnail. "Start taking pictures," Whitloe said to Samuels. "I'll be over here."

"He's like dead, like isn't he?" asked McMillan as Hunter Whitloe approached.

"Like *Totah*-ly." he replied, letting his professionalism slip for a moment. Without looking at the Valleyspeak kid to see if there came a response, Whitloe withdrew his notepad and pen from his pocket and began to write. "You discovered the body when?" he asked, not missing a beat.

"A little after seven. Maybe closer to, like, seven-ten." He looked over to the living room and appeared to become flustered. "Oh, I don't know."

Whitloe put his arm on the young man's shoulder and guided him over to the front door.

Crunch, crunch, crunch.

Ignoring the sound, he continued, "Let's start at the top. The show was about to go on the air." He ushered McMillan through the door, outside. "When does he usually get to the studio?"

"Around six-forty."

"Good." He made a note. "When did you start to get worried that he wouldn't show up?"

"About ten 'til," he replied, calmer. "The station manager called me into his office, and like, tore me a new asshole because Terry hadn't arrived. Then he 'suggested,'" he said, making quotation marks with his fingers, "I run over here 'to get his fat ass up.'"

Whitloe tried not to laugh. He coughed instead. "So you got here about. . ."

"Like I said, a little after seven. I like rang the doorbell, pounded on the door, and yelled for a good few minutes." He acted his way through the next part. "I like opened the screen door, nearly tripped over that fucking newspaper," he said pointing to the morning's edition of the *Times* he must have knocked into the nearby flower bed, "and came in here to find this." He walked in.

Crunch. Crunch, crunch. Crunch.

"Did you touch the body?" Whitloe asked, bracing himself for the worst. "Did you move anything?"

"Like, no fucking way, man. The guy was *dead*, you know?"

Whitloe made another note, thinking *Thank you, God.* "And you called 911 from. . ."

"From the phone in the kitchen."

"Anyone else?"

The young man paled. "Oh, God. I haven't called the TV station yet. Station manager's probably shittin' a brick."

"We'll handle it," the detective said, making a motion to Samuels to take care of it. "Did you notice anything strange, Mr. McMillan?"

"The guy is fucking dead, man. Isn't *that* strange enough for you?"

Whitloe slowed down. "I mean, did you see anyone nosing around? Did you notice anyone leaving when you arrived?"

"Nah," McMillan said. "Nothing like that."

"Meat wagon!" called a voice from the door. It was Deputy Coroner Tess Taggert. She came in. "What happened here, Hunter? Food fight?"

The detective spoke to Shannon McMillan once more before moving over to the coroner. "Have a seat in the kitchen, Mr. McMillan. I'll be back." On his way to the front door, Whitloe made a note to himself to check and see who the newspaper boy was for this area of town.

***

Tuesday morning, I caught sight of Otto Nicholson as he rounded the employee water cooler shortly after nine. I flipped to the ad I saw in the Entertainment section of yesterday's *Times* as I got his attention. "Here it is," I said, extending the paper. "This Saturday at the Regency in San Francisco. Can you make it?"

Otto pulled himself from distraction and focused on the ad. "Oh, the Con," he said. "Sure."

I had found out during one of our lunch time runs that Otto and I shared more than a passing interest in *Star Trek*, even though we were probably twice the average age of the typical Trekker. While my fascination lingered from the fantasy born in my early childhood, his centered on the scientific and technical aspects of the shows. He had confessed to having been to a number of Star Trek conventions. I, on the other hand, had not yet gone that far.

"But you'll have to drive," he added. "My car's still in the shop, and I might have trouble getting a news van on the weekend."

"No problem," I replied. "I can spring for your ticket, too, if you need me to," I said, imagining the cost of car repairs.

"No need for that. And let's just keep our little plan to ourselves, okay?"

I looked around to see if anyone had overheard our conversation. I had to admit my fandom sometimes embarrassed me, and — if exposed — could possibly resurrect the unflattering, bookish image

I'd maintained throughout my teens and on into undergrad school. I raised my right hand to my lips, letting out a "shhh," and quietly making the Vulcan hand sign for "Live long and prosper."

"Did you watch that morning exercise show on Public Access today?" Otto asked, changing the subject.

"No. I don't have cable. Why?"

"Oh, it's probably nothing," he said. "It's just that the show's host didn't make it in this morning, and they seemed to have to scramble to get someone to take his place."

"Maybe he overslept," I offered, easing myself into my chair and leafing through the day's assignments.

"I guess you're right. I'll just tune in tomorrow."

***

"Any word on the Matthew Black case?" Hunter Whitloe asked Deputy Coroner Tess Taggert. They had been at the Terry Totah crime scene for nearly four hours, having recently dismissed his assistant, Samuels, with the body. The exercise show's producer, Shannon McMillan, accompanied the deputy to have a set of his fingerprints taken at the Chestnut Grove police station since they were bound to show up on at least the kitchen telephone, and Whitloe didn't want to chase the kid down just so he could later rule out some stray latent.

"You're not going to like it," Taggert warned. "All signs point to choking, with the exception of a high concentration of nicotine in his system."

"'Nicotine'?" Whitloe echoed. "You mean like from cigarettes?"

"You got it. If he were trying to smoke and eat breakfast at the same time, a coughing fit could have easily led to choking on his cereal."

Whitloe tried to think. "I don't remember finding any cigarette butts at the scene, but I'll have to check my notes."

"That may not be necessary," the coroner said. "He didn't have to be smoking. If he was quitting, it could have been an early morning incident of Smoker's Cough. I remember having a rather bad case of it back before I quit."

"But what about the cereal?" the detective pressed. "And before you answer," he said, crunching around the living room for effect, "I suggest you look around. I'd say there's some connection."

"Maybe," Taggert said, "but I doubt it. We were able to find a small amount of Wheaties in the man's stomach, and to a greater degree, in his mouth and esophagus. He definitely had been eating the stuff, even if both you and I find that hard to believe. This, on the other hand," she continued, indicating Terry Totah's demise, "if it *did* involve foul play, could be the work of some copy-cat killer with a sense of humor who read one of the Black articles last week."

"Some sense of humor," Whitloe said.

"More likely a heart attack, Hunter. The man was getting up there, and he wasn't in the best of shape. His little program may have been more of a strain than he anticipated."

"Still, I think I'll check with his doctor to see what his medical history was. Hey," he said, making a note, "I'll check into Matthew Black's, too. You, meanwhile, keep me posted on anything you find with this one. I've got a bad feeling about this."

Whitloe returned to the Chestnut Grove police department around eleven-thirty, in time to see Deputy Jonathan Briggs pour half a glass of milk onto the bowl of cereal in front of him.

"Good morning, Lieutenant," Briggs said simply, picking up his spoon.

Whitloe stood there for a moment, wondering if the kid grew balls while he and Taggert were taping off the morning's crime scene. If Briggs had found out from Samuels the details of the earlier festivities, and how he had been quickly passed over to ride shot-gun, Whitloe could see how the young deputy might be pissed. He searched to see if this new sensation he was associating with Briggs might be a little bit of respect before he decided to speak.

"A little late for breakfast, isn't it, Briggs?"

Whitloe looked to the small box of Total — one of the 3" x 4" variety you'd find in a multi-pack — near the deputy's arm. At that moment, the detective noticed he was *smiling* at him. Now *that* was a first.

Briggs gave a small laugh. "Yeah, I guess so," he replied, blushing. "It was just getting late, and I was trying to wait for you for lunch, but I couldn't. Sorry." He picked up the Total box and said, "Luckily one of these samples came in the mail a few days ago, or I'd be starving." He hoisted a heaping spoonful of the cereal into his mouth and began to chew with glee.

Hunter Whitloe looked at him, and his thin smile faded. "'In the mail'? The cereal box came *in the mail* ?!" Storming over to the trash can alongside Briggs' desk, he rummaged through to find the remains of a small, brown wrapping that had obviously once enclosed the Total box. It had been postmarked five days ago. "You idiot!" he screamed as Briggs swallowed. "*You're eating evidence*!"

***

At the *Times*' Complaint Desk, the ever-cheerful Cindi Bates was looking anything but. She stressfully twisted a lock of her blond hair as she dutifully copied down the tirade coming from the other end of her phone.

Airheaded bitch, she wrote, next to the words, *CANCEL, CANCEL, CANCEL. Never ordered the rag* came next, along with a name: *Nicholas Pirelli.*

"That's *Councilman* Nicholas Pirelli," bellowed the voice, loud enough for Assistant News Editor Charlotte Journigan to hear as she walked by. Cindi began spelling: *C-O-U-N-C-I-L. . .*

"What's going on here?" Charlotte asked. She looked over Cindi's shoulder to her note, then took the receiver from the young girl. "Mr. Pirelli. . .?" she tried. Wincing, she pulled the phone from her ear as the man raged on.

"Now see here, *former* councilman," Charlotte interrupted. "There is no need to use that kind of language. . ." Again, she had to move the receiver away.

The commotion caught my attention, and I looked up from my copy to see that *Ms. Bitch* was not holding onto her patience.

"Listen to me, you syphilitic whore-monger," she said, snapping. "I will not tolerate your speaking to a member of my staff that way. If you don't want the fucking paper, we'll stop delivering it to that skanky hovel you call your home. I don't care whose fault it is, and I'm not going to debate it with your pompous, fat ass. Consider it done, and there will be no need for you to contact this office again." She paused. "'My name'?"

For half a second, I wondered how she would respond to that one.

"My name," she said in measured tones, "is Charlotte F. Journigan. Assistant News Editor. And unless you'd like to see another nice little article regarding your *manners* in the afternoon edition, you should shut your hole right this instant. I don't need some *former*, shamed politico trying to tell me how to run this paper or its circulation department. Now, thank you, and good bye."

I should have known, I thought, as she slammed down the receiver. A glance toward Otto Nicholson told me that now was not a good time to have any discussion about this.

Charlotte then bent down to the quivering Cindi Bates and said in soothing tones, "Be sure we do not deliver any further newspapers to Mr. Nicholas Pirelli. He never has seemed to appreciate our high journalistic standards anyway." Striking a match, she fired up a cigarette she pulled from a coat pocket, and took a long, satisfied drag. "And take the rest of the day off, dear. You look a little shaken. I think I'll be able to handle this phone if it rings again." With that, she strolled into her office and closed the door.

***

"Well," said Whitloe as he pulled up a chair across from his deputy's desk, "I guess we'll soon find out if it's the cereal that's poisoned."

"'Poisoned'?!" Briggs repeated while trying to spit out any bit of cereal that remained in his mouth. Frantically, he picked up the Total sample-size box then quickly spooned through the flakes in his bowl. Panic set in. "*Poisoned* ?" he said again.

"That's right, Briggs," Whitloe said calmly. "That just might be your last meal. You see, we found another dead guy in circumstances very similar to those of the late Matthew Black — you remember, last week's cereal *suicide* — this time, though, he'd been eating Total." He looked toward the deputy's snack and continued taunting, "Now what's that you've got in the bowl, Briggs?"

The deputy's mouth hung open for a moment as he followed Whitloe's gaze downward. "Oh, my God. Somebody do something!" He began to look around to the other officers as he picked up the phone. "Quick. The Poison Control Center. Wait, no, no. Call for an ambulance. Shit," he said without thinking, "what's the number for 911?!"

Of all the policeman in the vicinity, Hunter Whitloe was laughing the hardest. Of course he had known that the toxicology reports on the wheat flakes had shown nothing. Taggert had told him so.

"Relax, Briggs, relax," the detective said finally. Reluctantly, he filled in his rookie partner on the coroner's findings. "So unless this guy's radically changing his M.O., you should be okay. Just check with me before you eat any more cereal, understand?"

Briggs spit again. "I think I'm switching to bagels with cream cheese."

"Not a bad idea," Whitloe replied. He took a moment to reconstruct the Total box in its brown-paper wrapper. "No sense trying to lift prints from this," he noted, "but let's see just what else we can get from it."

When wrapped, the package was a simple 3" x 4" x 1-1/2" box. It had no return address (not that Whitloe had actually expected one), and in small, handwritten capitals was "CHESTNUT GROVE P.D.," the street, city, and zip. An adhesive strip for seventy-five cents from a mail metering machine served as postage, and the postal cancellation was local — Chestnut Grove — and done on February 18th, one day before Matthew Black was discovered.

"Looks like this joker's giving us some sort of advanced warning," speculated Whitloe. "How sporting of him."

"If that's the case, Lieutenant," interjected a now much calmer Briggs, "wouldn't we have gotten a box of Wheaties, too?"

He hated to admit it, but this kid had a point. "Unless you ate that, too," he countered in a foreboding tone.

The deputy closed his mouth tightly and shook his head in reply.

"All right, then," Whitloe said. "Then it has to be around here somewhere. Look over there."

Briggs and two other officers who had happened in on their conversation searched the immediate area around the deputy's desk and over to the copy machine. Whitloe moved over to the filing cabinets as the woman on afternoon dispatch came through and announced, "INCOMING!"

With a swing, she lifted her armful of incoming mail to shoulder-level, placing it in the metal IN-basket on top of the tallest filing cabinet. Her aim was off, however, and a number of envelopes slid over the top and down between the cabinet and the wall.

"Nice one, Shirl," Hunter Whitloe responded, bending over to pick up what she had dropped. It was then he saw the other 3" x 4" x 1-1/2" plain-wrapped package that had been lodged there. "Briggs, get me a letter opener or ruler," he said.

"Find something, Lieutenant?" he asked as he handed him a blue, plastic ruler.

"Just another piece to this puzzle, I think," Whitloe said. He carefully slid the package across the floor toward him, put on a pair of plastic gloves from a box nearby, and eased it to his sight line by holding the edges.

"Bingo," he said, taking the item over to his desk. "Same hand-lettered address, same kind of postage label, same brown packaging paper." Looking at the postmark, he read, "FEB 15, CHESTNUT GROVE, CA." He slid open his top drawer and located a retractable razor, then carefully slit enough of the wrapping to look inside. "'Wheaties,'" he said a little too enthusiastically. "Damn it." He rocked back in his padded chair for a moment as he thought things through. A moment later, he retrieved a plastic evidence bag from a side drawer and placed the cereal box inside it.

"Lieutenant?" It was Briggs again.

"What is it, Briggs? I'm trying to think." The detective turned to see the deputy simply pointing to the mail in-basket. There, half-buried under a large manila envelope, sat *another* 3" x 4" x 1-1/2", brown-wrapped box. Whitloe bolted from his chair and with his still-gloved hands lifted the package from the day's delivery.

With the care he had displayed before, Whitloe opened it. "'Trix,'" he said. "It's a fucking box of Trix."

"What could it mean?" asked Briggs.

It's a clue to who he's going to kill next, you idiot, Whitloe thought to himself. "I don't know, Briggs," he said instead. "I think I'll have to take this up with the Captain." As he rose with the latest package in one hand and the Wheaties box in the other, his mind raced: if this *were* some kind of clue, he thought, and judging from the postmarks on the first two boxes, he had about two or three days to figure it all out before he found out the hard way.

Chapter Four

Silly Rabbit. . .

"I THINK THAT BEFORE we go and invent a wheel, we should see if the cart really needs one, Hunter," Captain Colm Atherton said evenly.

"With all due respect, sir," Whitloe responded, "what more evidence do you want?" He indicated to the two brown-wrapped cereal boxes — now both sealed in plastic evidence bags until analyzed — on the desk, the third opened package that had been Briggs's mid-day snack, and his own notes and reports from the two recent crime scenes. "We've got two dead men here, three similar but rather odd packages sent an average of three days before a body turns up, and more fucking cereal than I'd now care to eat in my lifetime. I think. . ."

Just then, Briggs and Samuels entered, with the latter holding two photo envelopes, one marked "BLACK, M.," and the other "TOTAH, T.," with their respective case numbers stenciled in the corners. "I had 'em rush the Totah shots, Lieutenant. I haven't had a chance to look at them yet."

"That's fine, Samuels," the detective said. "Thanks." Opening the envelopes, he lay the pictures across the Captain's desk sequentially. After a while, he had run out of space but continued to stack them on top of each other, shot after shot after shot, for effect. "Here. . .and here. . .and here. . ."

"I took the first guy's," Deputy Jonathan Briggs said meekly.

"And here," Whitloe said, ignoring him. "And here. . .and here."

Atherton pulled a shot of Terry Totah, gagged with a mouthful of Total, from the stack, then he reached for one of Matthew Black, face-first in his cereal bowl, with the Wheaties box next to him.

Whitloe continued by picking up the small, packaged Wheaties in the evidence bag. "See? Sent Monday, February 15th," he said with a slight shake of the bag. He pointed to one of Briggs's photos and said, "Dead. Friday, February 19th." Moving to the other mailed package, he said, "Sent Thursday, February 18th," then to one of Samuels's shots, "Dead. Tuesday, February 23rd." Next came the Trix. "Sent Monday, February 22nd. . ."

"Dead," Captain Atherton followed flatly. "When?"

"My guess'd be Thursday or Friday," Whitloe said. "If he keeps to his pattern."

"More likely Friday," offered Briggs, to which Hunter Whitloe turned around, dumbfounded.

"Why Friday, Briggs?"

"Well," the deputy said slowly, "he mails the first box on a Monday. It's local, so it should get here the next day, Tuesday. The murder occurred on Friday. Three days later." He paused a moment for it to sink in. "The second box, the Total, is sent on Thursday. A day for mailing is Friday. And the next body is found the following Tuesday. . ."

"*Four* days later," Whitloe interrupted. "So much for that theory."

"Three *mail days*, Lieutenant," Briggs replied. "There's no mail delivery on Sundays. Three mail days would be the following Tuesday."

"'Mail days'?" Whitloe spat. "Of all the. . ."

"Why wouldn't the guy count Sundays?" asked the captain, agreeing with Briggs.

"Maybe he goes to church," said Whitloe sarcastically.

"Serial killers have been known to do weirder things, Lieutenant," noted the other deputy.

"*Et tu*, Samuels?" Whitloe said above a whisper.

"Maybe he wants to make sure we have time to get it," Briggs ventured. "The small cereal box, I mean. There is that connection."

"'Stop me before I kill again,'" Atherton toned.

"Well, at least he's polite," the detective said. "It's not just anybody who'll send out announcements before he commits a crime, let alone a murder."

Captain Atherton looked at Whitloe. "That's the part that doesn't have me convinced yet, Hunter. Are we really dealing with two *murders?* The coroner's office said Black choked to death, and you said Taggert's first impression of the Totah case was a heart attack. I'm not sure we have enough to go on."

"All the facts aren't in yet, sir," Whitloe said. "And given the high unlikelihood that these pre-death packages are nothing more than bizarre coincidences, I think we should do whatever we can to cover our asses."

"You wouldn't want to sit on this and have another stiff turn up, Captain," Deputy Samuels said.

Atherton was silent for a minute. "Okay men. I see your point." He looked down at the latest brown-wrapped package on his desk, and the three other men's gazes followed. "So, who's next?"

"Well," Whitloe said, thinking it through. "We have Wheaties for a former Olympic athlete; Total for the late Terry Totah — the man couldn't pronounce his "L's". . ."

But it was Jonathan Briggs who finished the thought, saying, "*Silly Rabbit. . .Trix are for kids.*"

***

After my lunch time run with Otto, I returned to my desk to find a telephone message from a friend and former colleague, Pamela Lawson. Pamela and I met when I was substitute teaching locally at Marshall Clancy High two years ago, and after suffering through a brief crush she had on me, as well as a few other adventures, we grew close. Over the course of our relationship, I'd lend an ear for her stories of troublesome students and education system politics, and she'd be there for the times I felt I was just spinning my wheels and needed to vent.

Together we'd complain about the problems of dating and speculate why neither of us could find a suitable man. Occasionally, I would accompany her to a single's club — "Meat racks," she'd call them — but she'd attract little attention because, I guess, I looked too much like a date. More often, she'd tag along with me to the town's gay bar, The Crystal Ball, on those nights I wanted to venture out of my small, in-law unit apartment, but didn't feel like cruising alone.

"Fag hag," I had once called her.

"I prefer 'fag *moll*,'" she'd replied, morphing a term used to describe a gangster's girlfriend.

Picking up the phone, I dialed the school's number and got the Main Office secretary. "Good afternoon, Mrs. White. It's Paul Blazer. I'm returning a call from Pamela Lawson. Could you page her for me?"

"Paul Blazer, well, I'll be," she said. "We were just talking about you. Principal Brandriff and I saw that article you wrote in last week's paper, you know, about Matthew Black. Tragic, really. Simply tragic. But we both agreed that the writing was just fine. You're moving up in the world."

"Thanks," I said a bit awkwardly. "You know, if now's not a good time, I can. . ."

"Oh, silly me. Just a minute, dear. Let me get her. She's in the History faculty workroom, between classes. One moment." There was a brief pause, then she returned to say, "Nice hearing from you. Keep up the good work."

"Thanks again, Mrs. White."

I could hear the receiver change hands, then, "Is this William Randolph Hearst?"

"Pamela, how are you? What's up?"

"Well, first, I called to say 'congratulations' on getting that article in the *Times* on that dead guy," Pamela said. "Mighty impressive. That's the first thing you've had published, isn't it?"

"Yeah, I guess so," I said, thinking about it. Silently I hoped that it didn't eat up all fifteen minutes of fame Andy Warhol had promised me. I wouldn't want that to be it.

"Great," she said. "Second, I was wondering if you were free tonight for dinner. We could celebrate your recent literary success."

"Sure. Come by around six."

"And third, how about joining me for a class on pepper spray?"

I laughed. Ever since that restaurant hostess had been murdered some two years back, Pamela had developed a penchant for brushing up on her self-defense skills, and pepper spray was the newest craze that threatened to replace mace. "We'll talk about it. But," I added, "don't get your hopes up."

"Do it, Paul. One day, you'll thank me for it."

"Pamela Lawson. . .my bodyguard," I toned. "See you around six."

"Bye."

***

At Captain Colm Atherton's insistence, Hunter Whitloe reluctantly divided some of the investigative work between himself and the two deputies, Samuels and Briggs. While he would follow up with the coroner's office on the latest results of the Totah autopsy, Samuels took the single-serving-sized cereal boxes over to the Criminalistics Lab in Martinez for analysis. Fearing some major screw-up from the department's youngest deputy, the detective had Briggs do something relatively simple as well as foolproof: check with the town's two post offices for any recollection of someone mailing three particular packages measuring 3" x 4" x 1-1/2".

"Where's Taggert?" Whitloe asked the number two medical examiner, Redford Malone, as he walked into the coroner's office some time around twelve-thirty.

"Grabbing a bite to eat, I'd suspect," Malone replied. "She should be back in about an hour. What can I do for you, Lieutenant?"

"What's the word on the Totah case?"

Malone gestured Whitloe down the hallway. "Come see for yourself. I've been working on him since he was brought in this morning."

Terry Totah's body lay on the steel autopsy table, Y-cut and partially dissected, with body fluids still dripping through the numerous holes in the table's surface. Assorted viscera — the heart, lungs, esophagus, and trachea — had been removed *en bloc* and were separated onto individual plastic sheets for examination.

"I haven't gotten to the liver, spleen, adrenals, and kidneys," he said, pointing to the open body cavity. "But they're next. I suspect the study of the stomach, pancreas, and intestines will be routine, so I probably won't get to them until later this afternoon or tomorrow."

"'Routine'?" echoed the detective. "Why 'routine'?"

"Well, the cereal he came in with — Total, if I'm not mistaken — didn't make it past the back of his mouth." He picked up a scalpel and metal dissecting pin and trained Whitloe's attention on the segmented trachea and esophagus. He could see that both were free from any trace of the breakfast food. "That would almost definitely rule out any form of ingestible poison, since without digestion the substance would have to have been so caustic that it would have virtually destroyed the mouth." A quick inspection of Totah's mouth showed no damage.

"So you won't find any cereal in his digestive system," Whitloe said. "Routine," he said again.

"Exactly. We'll do the standard tests on the contents and fluids removed from the stomach as well as the mouth, of course, but I wouldn't count on much."

Whitloe looked back at the body. "So what killed him?"

"Judging from the extent of the necrosis of the heart tissue, I'd say you've got a standard M.I."

Whitloe gave Malone a look. "English, please."

"Sorry," he said. "Myocardial infarction."

"Heart attack," Whitloe said, shaking his head. "It just doesn't make sense."

"I'll have them rush the toxicologicals," Malone said, trying to fish for some good news. "It won't take the usual week. I'd say tomorrow or Thursday."

"Make it tomorrow if you can," Whitloe urged. He thought of his time table. "Thursday may be too late."

"You got it. I'll have Taggert call if there's anything out of the ordinary in the results."

"Thanks, Malone." The detective thought for a moment. "What does the press know of this? Any idea?"

"They know he's dead," the coroner said. "I overheard Tess talking with someone from Channel Five earlier. It'll probably make the 6 o'clock news."

"She told them *heart attack*, didn't she? No mention of the cereal?" Whitloe mentally crossed his fingers.

"That's right," Malone confirmed. "The cereal wasn't an issue. He just keeled over while having breakfast, that's all."

I don't think so, thought Whitloe. "Thanks for your time. Tell the doc I was by, will you?"

"Sure thing," he said. "Now I guess it's back to work." And with that, Redford Malone donned a pair of rubber gloves and thrust his hands back into the chest of Terry Totah. He didn't look up to see the detective walk out the door.

In Martinez, Deputy Samuels was getting a crash course on the sheriff's department's newest piece of crime-fighting equipment from criminologist Sydney Pincus.

"It's called the Alternative Light Source, or ALS for short," Pincus said. "It's a $15,000 portable system that with a special light and goggles can work wonders."

Samuels stared at what looked like some high-tech vacuum cleaner with a special hose from which a light shined.

"By passing this hose along a wall or other surface where some elusive bit of evidence might be," Pincus explained, demonstrating the device on a bit of fabric from a recent rape case, "what was once hidden now shines." As he did so, a partial fingerprint on the elastic waistband and what appeared to be numerous semen stains shimmered when viewed through the special goggles. "Cool, huh?"

"Impressive," Samuels said. "How does it work?"

"It filters out all but one color of light in the visible spectrum," the criminologist said. "When you wear different colored goggles, evidence pops out in astonishing detail. Different colors highlight different kinds of evidence: blood, semen, fingerprints, old bite marks, bruises. . ."

"How about trying the ALS on a couple of things I brought along with me?" Samuels asked. He could sense that Pincus was more than a little eager to play with his new toy, so he expected little resistance. Carefully, he produced the small boxes of Wheaties and Trix from their evidence bags.

"What?" Pincus asked. "Don't tell me Count Chocula's turned to a life of crime and joined forces with the Frito Bandito!"

What's the number for 911?! Deputy Jonathan Briggs thought to himself, with a mental kick to the head. He was pulling into the parking lot of the second Chestnut Grove's two post offices, replaying the earlier events of the morning along the way.

What a sap! he nearly said aloud.

Of all of his shortcomings, Briggs was most aware — usually in hindsight alone, however — of his uncanny ability to speak first, think later. His gaff about 911 was only the most recent example.

Once he had called the toll-free computer hot line when his terminal had prompted him to "HIT ANY KEY," and after about twenty minutes of searching his keyboard, he complained to the telephone technician that nowhere could he find the "ANY" key.

On another occasion, he rushed to the nearest post office to buy a bunch of stamps "before they went up to 29 cents," as he had announced to the entire precinct. That little incident haunted him to this day.

"Hey, Briggs," one fellow officer would say, "they had a rush on 25-cent stamps today. Did you get yours yet?"

Or, "Hey, John, how many stamps can you get for a dollar?"

This little faux pas had somehow even made its way back to his family, and one day he arrived at the station to find a pink telephone message on his desk from his mother that read: "Wants you to stop at the P.O. on your way home. *Needs stamps*."

Fortunately, he was good-natured enough to take these jibes in fun and with the affection they were intended, but there were times like today when he sensed an underlying sting that would serve as a reminder for the young officer to slow things down and think before engaging his mouth. And wherever he was low in what his father termed "book smarts," he usually made up for in common sense and the more practical "street smarts," the two things that could often mean the difference between life and death in his chosen line of work.

Just slow down a little, Briggs, and you'll do fine, he told himself.

He hoped to use his current assignment — tracing the postage label on the cereal boxes — to shore up the confidence of his peers. The Lieutenant *and* the Captain had given him this task, after all. If he pulled this off, he would win big.

After holding the heavy glass door open for an elderly woman as she left, Briggs took his place at the end of the post office line, five customers deep. In his hand, he fidgeted with the re-wrapped Total box and the adhesive postage label that he had removed and slid into a plastic sheath. When he reached the head of the line, he tried to endear himself to the frumpy, female postal worker who stood before him.

Looking at a picture on the wall, he said, "Gee. Mighty rough looking fellow. One of the Ten Most Wanted?"

The woman, branded "HODGEKINS" by her name tag, followed his stare, then turned to report, "That's Mr. Woodbridge. He's our Employee of the Month."

***

Otto Nicholson strode over to my desk and plopped a copy of the *San Francisco Chronicle* in front of me. "I've got to have these *now*," he said, with an index finger toward an article titled, "Hillside Strangler Sues Over Crime Cards."

"Otto," I warned, "this is the *Chronicle*. You know Ms. Journigan's rule about copies of the competition in the newsroom." The Assistant News Editor had imposed a moratorium on having recent issues of the other Bay Area newspapers around when one of her cub reporters had been accused of plagiarism by a larger, more powerful publishing magnate. An issue of even *The National Enquirer* could be considered taboo, carrying with it a day's suspension or possible termination, if it were a multiple offense.

Nicholson made a sound that told me he couldn't care less about some silly rule. "Scooped again, Blazer. It's just par for the course with this old paper. But never mind that," he said with a gesture back to the article, "these things are *big*."

The article detailed a recent lawsuit filed by Kenneth Bianchi, the convicted serial killer better known as the Hillside Strangler, against a Sonoma County publishing company that had produced a series of True Crime, bubble-gum-styled trading cards and used an image of the murderer without his permission. Bianchi was suing for two million dollars, calling on the company to share its profits with him.

"This is a little ludicrous, don't you think?" I asked.

"Of course it is," Nicholson replied, "but can you imagine what these things would be worth after something like this?"

I wondered, remembering the rash of criticism that flared up when the cards first appeared last June. Police officers and the families of the killer's victims pushed elected officials from several states to draft legislation to ban them even before the first sets appeared in stores. If I recalled correctly, the group, Eclipse Comics, was planning two more sets in the series, as well as a run of AIDS-related cards that would highlight famous doctors, researchers, and sufferers of the disease, with a condom in each pack instead of bubble gum. I still hadn't decided how I felt about that one.

"Where do you think you'll find them?" I asked.

"At the Con on Saturday. Dealers and collectors of all kinds set up booths at those things. We'd have to hit them early."

"If you do find a set," I suggested, "maybe we can road trip to a few of the prisons and have some of the guys autograph them for you."

The look Otto gave me next said that he was actually entertaining the thought, until he realized I was just kidding with him. "Not bad, Blazer. You had me going there."

"And you *me*."

"Hey, when you write obituaries as long as I have, stuff like this takes on a little fascination, you know," he said. "Allow me just one idiosyncrasy, will you?"

"Okay, okay. Just watch it with that paper. Here she comes."

We looked up to see Charlotte Journigan step out of her office to hand one of the journalism co-op students from the local community college a couple of dollars to run and get her a pack of cigarettes. Otto picked up the forbidden paper, folded it under his arm, and gave me a wink.

"Gotta run to the pet shop after work today," he said. "My octopus came in. Want to tag along?"

"Sorry," I said. "I'm meeting a friend for dinner. Maybe next time."

"No problem. I'll catch you later." With that, he turned and left.

***

"Give me some good news," Detective Hunter Whitloe ordered Deputy Samuels later that afternoon. With his first follow-up at the medical examiner's office a bust, he needed something to cheer him up.

"We've got a partial print from the Trix box," he said, "and at first glance, it may be similar to the latent you lifted from Matthew Black's neck. If the guy's using rubber gloves, they're pretty thin, and he doesn't know it. Pronounced friction ridges help, too."

"So there *is* a connection," Whitloe murmured.

"Possibly," the deputy cautioned. "They're still running the majority of the prints through AFIS," he said, meaning the Automated Fingerprint Identification System, "and that may take a couple of weeks, if they get a match at all."

"Damn," the detective said.

"What's the word on the autopsies or Briggs's postal label?"

Before Whitloe could relay any of his own disappointments, Jonathan Briggs entered the station through a side door, followed by a young, female uniformed officer, with a "Probation Department" patch on her chest and her blond hair tucked up under a matching cap.

"What'd you come up with, Briggs?" asked the detective.

The deputy gave a slight wave. "Hey, Lieutenant. This is Bedilla Burton, from Juvenile Hall. I ran into her at the post office over on Westport. She was mailing a package to her folks. Imagine that."

The thin, young woman extended a hand toward Whitloe, saying, "Call me 'Birdie.' Everyone else does."

Ignoring her hand as well as all social pleasantries, Whitloe glared at Briggs. "And what were you supposed to be doing at the post office, Briggs? Do you remember?"

"Oh," the deputy said. "The postage label. Well, I spoke with a few clerks at both stations, and no one remembered anyone coming in to mail our little cereal packages."

"That's where I came in," Birdie Burton added.

Whitloe redirected his attention to the officer from Juvenile Hall, now with a little more interest. "Oh, do tell."

"Looking at the label itself," she said, "it seems to be printed on a standard adhesive-backed paper on an ordinary mail metering machine, the kind many businesses now use, or even places like a Kinko's copy center."

"Great," Whitloe said. "There must be a hundred of them in this town."

"Actually," Briggs replied, "there are only two Kinko's and one major supplier of office products. Birdie and I could hit those places in no time, and if the supplier keeps records of who has bought postage machines, we can check them out, too."

"Get on it," the detective said simply. It wasn't the worst news he'd had today, and so far, this lead wasn't becoming monumental.

Briggs smiled and with a turn, he escorted Probation Officer Burton out the door.

"What about the killer's next victim, Lieutenant?" Samuels asked. "Shouldn't we be looking into that as well?"

"Shhh," the detective said, bringing a finger to his lips. He leaned in the direction of the younger deputy's departure to be sure he had left earshot, then said, "Watch it, Samuels. If we can keep those two busy, it keeps them out of our hair."

"Gotcha," Samuels said.

Whitloe smiled, happy that he had actually sensed a bit of rivalry between the two officers earlier. "Now, let's put our heads together, and see what we can come up with."

***

At about ten to six, I heard a light rapping on my apartment door. Pulling an old college T-shirt over my head, I crossed the entire floor of the place in little over four steps. The dog, who'd been laying against the door, got up and padded over to my futon, where he promptly sprawled out.

"Off the bed," I said to him as I opened the door, to which he only responded with a slight move of his head and a playful growl.

"Listens as well as ever, I see," Pamela Lawson noted, stepping inside.

I decided to try something. "*Stieg aus das Bett* !" I said, wondering if I was remembering my high school German correctly.

"What?"

I guess the dog understood me, even if Pamela didn't, because an instant later, Dante got up off the futon and sat on the carpet beside it. With a little cock of the head, he stared at me, wondering what I would say next.

"What the hell was that?" Pamela asked.

I gave Dante a soothing scratch on the ear. "The dog and I have finally come to some understanding," I said with a smile. "So, where are we going?"

Giving me the once over, she said, "Apparently nowhere nice like Ellenbogen's Bistro, the way you're dressed."

"What's wrong with the way I'm dressed?" I asked, looking at the T-shirt and blue jeans combination I had on.

"I thought we were going out to celebrate your story being published. I really hadn't planned on doing it in a McDonald's."

"Fine," I conceded. With a tug, I had the shirt off, then was rummaging through my closet. "But the jeans stay. I have to wear my dress pants all day."

"Oh, all right. Have it your way."

I took out an off-white, long-sleeved cotton shirt with banded collar and a cotton/acetate, three-buttoned vest with an Aztec print on its front. "How's this?"

Pamela was looking approvingly, but not at my latest choice of clothing "Are you sure you're not straight?" she asked.

I flexed my biceps just to tease her a little more and said, "Never had it; never will." A moment later, I had slipped on the shirt and was buttoning it up. "Better?"

"Much. How's Chevy's?" she suggested, naming the town's latest Ameri-Mexican franchise that opened at the first of the year.

"Sounds good to me. Attack mode, Dante," I said, picking up my keys, and heading for the door. Just then, the phone rang.

As I pulled the door shut, locking it, Pamela asked, "Aren't you going to get that?"

"Nah. The machine'll pick it up." As we walked to the car, I could faintly hear my voice come on:

Hi. You've reached Paul Blazer at 686. . .

I waited for Pamela to get situated in the passenger seat of my candy-apple red Jeep Wrangler, then I started the engine. Then we were flying down Cedarbrook Crescent, to the end of my neighborhood, and on into the heart of downtown Chestnut Grove.

***

". . .reached Paul Blazer at. . ."

Otto Nicholson waited for the answering machine to finish before toning in, "Paul, this is Otto. If you're there, pick up. If you're not picking up and you're there, turn on the Channel Five news. Remember that public access fitness instructor I mentioned this morning at work? Well, apparently he's dead. Heart attack, or something. So I guess he won't be on the program tomorrow. Just thought you'd want to know. No real need to call me back tonight. I'll see you in the morning. Bye."

***

"I'll be back with that pitcher of margaritas in just a minute," our waitress promised.

"Thanks," I said. "And thanks for dragging me out once again, Pamela. I was beginning to get a little stir-crazy."

Pamela gave me a look as she dipped a tortilla chip into the small bowl of salsa. "Don't give me that, Blazer. You always managed to lead a far more interesting life than I do. So, how are things going between you and that young man from the bar?"

"Who, Davin?" I said. "Not much, really."

Davin and I had met shortly after I had gotten to know Pamela, back in 1991. He was a close friend to a certain local drag performer named Ruby Slippers, who had taken an immediate liking to me when I moved into town. I had gone out with Davin rather consistently for about six months — to the point that my small circle of gay friends knew us as a couple — but things cooled off shortly thereafter, although we would still manage to get together once or twice a month since then.

"We're still friendly," I explained. "I mean, we still see each other from time to time, but he's only twenty-three. And I'll be twenty-nine in four months."

"Ooo, one shy of the Big Three-Oh. You *are* old. Have you started searching for a burial plot?"

I tried to laugh, but I couldn't. I had seen a handful of friends and acquaintances die earlier than they should have, given the times we live in, and dying young no longer had the glamour it once might have had.

Pamela must have caught on to what I was thinking because she quickly apologized. "I'm sorry, Paul," she said. "Sometimes I forget the specter you live under."

"We all do, Pamela."

"I know that," she said, now getting uncomfortable. She tried to change the subject. "So, when's your next article due out?"

I looked at her, unready to move on. "You don't have to tip-toe around this subject, Pamela. And actually, there's something else I've been wanting to get off my chest."

Her look turned grave.

I knew what she was thinking: that I was dying. "Listen," I said, not wanting to toss the seriousness out of the conversation. "I got a Christmas card from my ex in Los Angeles, and he told me he's tested HIV positive."

"Oh, Paul, that terrible," she said, but the tone in her voice, and in what she said next, betrayed her relief. "But that was, what, *four years ago*, and you've been tested since then, haven't you?"

"Yes," I said, realizing that this was not the way I had wanted this to go. How could I convey the sadness I had felt when I had read Scott's letter last December? Of course I hadn't been with him in four years, but it didn't mean I no longer cared for him. "Like clockwork; every six months."

"And everything's okay, isn't it? I'm sure it is, or you wouldn't get tested every six months, right?"

"Right."

How could I say that whenever anyone I knew turned up positive, it wasn't easy. God, the two weeks you waited for the results were agony, regardless of the last test, or how safely you had played since then.

"So, everything's all right then," she said, with a little more finality in her tone than I would have liked.

"I guess," I said, trying to find the right words. "I just wanted to say that I'm going in for another test tomorrow, and I wanted somebody to know about it. And I wanted that someone to be you." Before she could respond, I wanted to simply slap myself because that didn't sound anything like what I wanted to say. To avoid the overt sentimentality that would surely follow, I added, "I should have the new results in two weeks. On March ninth."

At that time, our waitress returned with our pitcher of margaritas and two frosted glasses with salt. "Here you go. Your food should be up in just a few minutes."

Pamela took the pitcher and filled both glasses, sliding one over to me. "Here's to good news," she said, raising her glass. "Although I know things are going to be fine."

I smiled, then took a long sip of the drink, thinking, sadly, *And none of that ever matters.*

"Well, things at the high school are as hectic as ever," she said. "You know, since you left, I've been sentenced to be adviser for the school newspaper. . ."

"Ah, *The Clancy Chronicle*," I interrupted. "I remember it well."

"And aside from deadlines, we're coming up on mid-terms and the Prom in May. And on Friday, we've got an all-school assembly, and you-know-who's been recruited as one of the faculty monitors."

"Good for you," I said, without sympathy, for I knew that regardless of the complaining, she really did love what she was doing. "What's this year's event about?"

"We've got a former Marshall Clancy grad — Class of '89 — who killed three other kids his age halfway through last summer. DUI. As part of his probation, he's to do community service by going around to schools in the Bay Area to talk of the dangers of drinking and driving."

"Well, at least something good's coming out of all of it. Good for all those kids."

"And it's a big to-do, too," she said. "The principal wanted an extra two photographers from the student paper, and the local media's been notified. There's no telling just who may show up."

"Sounds like you've got your hands full. Whenever do you find time to date?"

"Ah, now *that's* another story. . ."

The food came, and we spent the better part of the evening together, catching up. After the second pitcher of margaritas, I was able to convince her that I really didn't need a class in the handling of pepper spray but told her to be sure to let me know how it went. Around eleven, I took her home, then got back to my apartment with just enough energy to walk Dante before I went to bed.

I didn't notice the message light flashing on my answering machine as I turned off the light and stripped down to my briefs to slide under the sheets.

***

"You're getting in rather late, dear," Gladys Whitloe called from the bed as her husband came quietly into the bedroom. "It's nearly midnight."

Whitloe only offered a grunt in reply, and he began to undress.

"I heard on the news about Terry Totah," she said. "That's why you ran out of here in such a hurry this morning, isn't it?"

To that, there was no response, leaving her to think, "Bore and gore. Bore and gore." He'd be up all night again, she suspected, poor man. She tried to get him to think about other things by saying, "Geneva Todd called to remind us about the bridge game on Sunday," to which Hunter gave a simple "Uh-huh."

"And your brother called from New York at about seven o'clock our time," she said. "I guess that's around ten where he is."

"Clayton?" Whitloe asked.

"That's right. He'd like you to call him."

"I'll bet he does," Hunter said. Without another word, he crawled beside his wife and turned off the small bedside light she had left on for him.

"Now Hunter. How long are you going to let this thing go on?"

"It's between my brother and me, Gladys," he said, facing the darkness with his back toward her. "I don't want to hear any more about it, understand?"

"But I think. . ."

He rolled over on his back. "I know what you think, dear," he said, trying not to let any anger creep into his voice. "But it doesn't make any difference this time. It's something I have to work out on my own. If I ever do. Now, it's been a very trying day, so good night." With that, he gave her a kiss and turned back on his other side, away from her.

She was able to lie next to him until about one-thirty, when his twitching and tossing drove her to the sofa in the living room.

Chapter Five

Nuttin', Honey

ALTHOUGH I HAD BEEN pretty beat after my evening out with Pamela Lawson, the thought of my afternoon appointment at the anonymous HIV-testing facility in nearby Walnut Creek had kept me from getting a decent night's sleep. In fact, it was a sudden panic attack that woke me about an hour before my alarm was set to go off at 6:30, immediately putting me in a foul mood.

Dante seemed happy to have me up a little earlier than usual though, and he crawled up to lie on top of me, licking my face, until I relented and took him on a pre-dawn jog around the neighborhood.

"I hope you're happy," I said to him, as I stripped off my damp tank top and gray sweats and started the shower. He gave his tail a steady wag in reply. But the run, the water, and the mist did little to lessen the anxiousness that awoke me, and toweling off, I resigned myself to a long day ahead.

"Get my message?" asked Otto Nicholson when I arrived at the *Times*.

I poured some hot water into my coffee mug for some tea and placed it in the microwave. "'Message'? No, Otto, sorry. I guess I forgot to check my answering machine. You called?"

He gave me the gist of his telephone call, filling me in on the death of local fitness guru Terry Totah. Retrieving my mug, I tossed in a tea bag and a packet of Sweet-n-Low, and together we walked back to my desk.

"A call came in late yesterday from the show's producer," Otto said. He looked around my desk until he found the pink message sheet. "Shannon McMillan," he read, "wants you to call him. The cast and crew of 'Total Fitness' want to chip in for his obituary since he has no real family to speak of."

"That's pretty thoughtful of them," I noted, "but writing the notice is your job, Otto. Shouldn't. . .?"

With a smile, he waved me on. "You can handle this one. After last week's article on Matthew Black, you're probably hungry for something else to write, and since Charlotte isn't exactly breaking down your door with a new assignment, I thought I'd do something to help out. Keep you busy."

"Thanks," I said.

"Just let me know if you need any help," he said, returning to his desk and the stack of papers on it.

I picked up my phone and punched the number on the message sheet.

***

Lieutenant Detective Hunter Whitloe flipped through his pages of notes in the Black and Totah files, looking for what would be his next step. Deputy Samuels sat patiently on the other side of his desk. Briggs had not yet come in.

"I'd still like to get my hands on the medical records of these two," Whitloe said. "See if there's any pre-existing condition we need to know about."

"Like being prone to choking on breakfast cereal," Samuels said, to which the detective responded with an angry stare. "Sorry, sir. I'll take Totah if you want Black. That shouldn't be too difficult."

"Fine. You may have to flash a badge and lean a little to get past that doctor-patient confidentiality bullshit, but I'm sure you can handle it."

"Good morning, Lieutenant," said Deputy Jonathan Briggs. "Sorry I'm late, but Birdie and I were up for a while last night going over what we still needed to cover with those postage labels. Both Kinko's were a bust, but the office supply store gave us about twenty places we have yet to check out. I'm meeting her in half an hour down at Probation. You don't mind if she helps out, do you, sir?"

Whitloe shook his head, thinking, *You need all the help you can get, Briggs.* "No," he said instead. "Just keep me posted."

"I sure wish there was more I could do to help," the young officer said.

"You're doing just fine, Briggs," Whitloe said. With a glance toward the other deputy, he continued, "And that postage label is one of the strongest leads we've got, so take it as slow as you need to. I want a thorough job here."

"Yes sir," Briggs said with a smile. "I won't let you down."

As he turned to leave, Samuels gave a concerned look and said, "Lieutenant, what's wrong with your chin?"

"Nothing," Whitloe said almost immediately. He brought up his right hand to rub it, saying, "You'd better get going, too, Samuels."

"Sure, Lieutenant."

The detective got up and turned toward the Captain's office as he heard his other deputy trail off in the direction of the station's front door. Catching a glimpse of himself in the reflection of a pane of glass, he noticed the faint, red wrinkle in the center of his chin that showed up whenever he tried to lie. Quietly, he was glad that his wife wasn't here to see it.

Jonathan Briggs was nearly knocked off his feet as he came through the double glass doors of the Probation Department at Juvenile Hall. An angry teenager in a faded high school letterman jacket had bolted from his chair to make a break for it when his latest meeting with his probation officer didn't go exactly as planned.

"Stop him," someone called out. "Don't let him leave here."

Briggs responded instinctively with a leg and slamming motion that tripped the young man into the wall with the deputy right behind him. He wrenched the kid's left arm behind his back, giving it a painful tug to assure him he wasn't going anywhere.

"Thanks, Briggs," Birdie Burton said. She came up and produced a pair of handcuffs, which she used quickly and efficiently. "You've messed up one time too many, Donovan," she said to the teen as she turned him around. She passed him to two other male officers waiting for him. "And I don't think you'll just get a slap on the wrist this time."

Briggs took a seat near Birdie Burton's desk and said simply, "Rough morning."

"Some kids never learn, I guess," she replied.

"He really didn't look like a kid."

"He's not. Not any more, anyway. He'll be twenty in a couple of months, but he's been on probation since he was seventeen. When he was convicted, he came through Juvi. For continuity, we like to keep them with the same P.O.," she explained, using the abbreviated term for probation officer. "It usually helps them along."

Briggs trained his eyes on the cuffed teen and his two uniformed escorts. "Not this time," he said. "Too bad."

"All in a day's work, Deputy," Birdie replied. "But you can't let it get to you. For every one like P.J. Donovan, there's usually two or three like this one."

She handed Briggs an interoffice memo, detailing one of the probation department's recent success stories. It even had a picture of the kid, named Artie Kellogg, although the Xerox quality made his face almost indiscernible.

"Artie was convicted on three counts of vehicular manslaughter last summer," she said. "Driving Under the Influence. He's been a saint since then, making my job with him that much easier. He now goes around and preaches the evils of drinking and driving to high school kids, so everybody's getting something out of it." She pointed to the line at the bottom of the flier. "He'll be at Marshall Clancy High on Friday."

Jonathan Briggs put the memo back on Burton's desk. "Three cheers for the system," he said sincerely. "It does work sometimes, doesn't it?"

"When we let it," she said. "Now, I've been able to arrange my rounds around your little errands, so if you can wait half a minute while I finish this report, we'll be on our way."

"Sure," Briggs said. During the next few minutes, as she typed her report, he looked over his list of companies that had bought a certain type of postage label machine, trying to decide where *his* next success would be.

***

"Blazer, in my office NOW!"

Charlotte Journigan's command was so loud and so sudden, I jumped an inch or two off my seat when I heard it. I scooped up a pen and pad in record time, sending a look Otto's way to see if he knew what was going on. He shrugged his shoulders.

"She sounds kind of angry," I said in a voice above a whisper.

"Blazer!"

This second call stopped everyone in the area who hadn't paused the first time. I tried to avoid eye contact with any of them, and I headed straight for the Assistant News Editor's office.

"Is something wrong?" I asked, moving to take the chair directly across from her desk.

"Close the door," she said. "And don't sit down."

I did as ordered and stood before her, trying not to seem nervous. I could tell that it wasn't working.

"Paul, who's the Assistant News Editor around her?"

"You are," I answered. *Where was this going*? I wondered.

"And who oversees your position and gives you your assignments?"

"You do."

"Then tell me," she said, with no trace of her Southern accent remaining, "what were you working on this morning, and who told you to do it?"

Uh-oh, I thought. The Totah obit. "I was following up on a call from the Contra Costa Public Access television station for an obit on Terry Totah, the fitness instructor who passed away yesterday."

"I know that fat fuck died yesterday," she yelled. "What were *you* doing returning the call? *I* didn't tell you to, did I?"

"Charlotte, I was doing the standard follow-up. I thought that was my job. I decided to help Otto out." No sense dragging him into this, I thought, deciding to temper the truth. He had no idea what a stink this would cause.

She lit a cigarette and took a strong drag, sucking away about half of it, then, as she exhaled, she threw it into her cup half-filled with water. She glared at me through the cloud of smoke for another half a minute before she spoke again. "I haven't cleared you in making calls. You're strictly morguework at the moment. You'll get larger responsibilities when I've decided you're capable of handling them, and not before. Understand me?"

"I'm sorry, Charlotte. I was just. . ."

"I asked if you understood me, Blazer," she interrupted.

"Yes, ma'am," I said.

"Now, I want you to gather all your notes on the Totah obit, and give them to Laney," she said, mentioning one of the community college co-ops who I'd seen around. "She'll take it from there."

"Yes, ma'am," I said. She was doing this as some sort of punishment, and I had to admit that it effectively added insult to injury. "Anything else?" I asked, hoping to get me out of there as soon as possible.

"Yes," she said. "If you find yourself about to do anything on the job that you remotely think might be out of the ordinary, you'd better clear it with me first. I won't tolerate anything like this happening again."

"Fine." I turned to leave.

"And here," she added, handing me her Taco Bell cup ashtray. "Give this to Nicholson when you see him. Have him toss it and bring me another."

I took the cup without a word and headed out of her office.

"Close the door behind you."

I did.

"You should see my octopus," Otto said during our lunch time run. "It's got the most beautiful blue markings amid its brown-speckled skin.

It's eyes are almost cat-like, and he seems to be rather intelligent. I had to add a tank separator to keep him from eating the other fish, but I wouldn't be surprised if he figures some way out of it. And because of the shape of his head, I've named him 'Bullwinkle.' It kind of looks like a moose."

Otto had thankfully managed not to bring up my brow-beating from Charlotte, although I could tell he knew something was up. His idle chat as we jogged into our second mile gave me some personal space that someone else wouldn't necessarily afford me. Silently, I thanked him for that, and I knew I could bring it all up when *I* felt ready to talk about it.

"I'd. . .like to. . .see it sometime. . ." I panted. "Maybe Saturday . . . before the Con."

"That reminds me," he said. "Were you planning to go in costume?"

"I hadn't. . .really thought about it," I said. "Are you?"

"Would you think me a complete geek if I did?"

"No. . .It might. . .be kind of fun."

Otto smiled, "I knew you would play along. I've got a complete, regulation Starfleet uniform from *The Next Generation*, fourth season. Command red. Captain's pips. And a working comm-badge and phaser."

I laughed. "Captain Nicholson. Well. . .that's a little. . .much for me. . .but I think. . .I have a pair of. . .Vulcan ears. . .from a costume party. . .a few years back. Maybe. . .I can find them."

"We can put you in a gangster suit, and you can go as Spock from that classic Trek episode called 'A Piece of the Action.' Star Date 4598.0."

"All I need's. . .a Tommy-gun."

"I think I can dig one of those up," he said. "And we'll have to get you the hair."

I ran my hands through my sweaty flattop. "I guess. . .you have. . .that, too. . ."

"I've got a trunkful of stuff that'd make Mr. Mott proud," he said, naming the blue-faced barber from *The Next Generation*. "We'll set you up."

"Sounds. . .like fun. . ."

"Enough talk," Otto said. "Concentrate on your breathing. You're getting winded."

I did as I was told but found myself thinking about my run-in with Charlotte. *God, I wish this day would be over.* Then I remembered my clinic appointment this afternoon and felt even worse.

***

Jonathan Briggs could hardly contain himself.

"Lieutenant!" he called out, bursting into the station around 3:45. Birdie Burton trailed at his heels. "Lieutenant!"

Captain Colm Atherton walked out of his office to quiet the deputy. "He's out, Briggs. Checking on a lead in the Black case. So's Samuels. Now, tell me what all this is about."

Briggs doubled over for a moment to catch his breath. He and Burton had sprinted almost all the way from the parking lot, barely able to contain the excitement they shared when it came to them. Straightening up, he reached into his back pocket and pulled out a sheet of paper that had been quickly folded into fourths. He was shaking.

"We've got it," he said, explaining nothing. "We — Birdie and I — were just standing in the middle of an insurance agent's office, you know, checking out one of those postal label machines, when BAM! It just came to me. Like a flash out of nowhere." He shook the piece of paper and smiled.

"Slow down, Briggs," the Captain said. "Slow down. You still haven't said a damn thing. What came to you?"

"This," he said, extending his arm. "We've figured out who's next!"

To be more productive, Captain Atherton had escorted both Briggs and Burton into his office. He stood patiently as the young deputy paced back and forth in front of his desk.

"Artie Kellogg," Briggs said. He handed the Probation Office flier about the young man on community service work for DUI. "Kellogg," he repeated. "Get it? And he's a *kid*. Well, practically. 'Silly Rabbit. . .Trix are for *kids*.' And he'll be speaking at an assembly full of kids on Friday, the day we expect another murder. Friday."

Atherton looked at the piece of paper then to Birdie Burton. "What do you know of this?" he asked her.

"It all makes sense, sir," she said. "Kellogg's due at Marshall Clancy High in the morning for two programs. They can't get the whole student body in the auditorium at one time. Since his family moved out of the area shortly after his accident last year, he's staying in a hotel in town. The Sheraton, I think. Part county expense, but he upgraded to a better place on his own. He checked in today at two, then called his probation officer to say he made it."

"And you agree with Briggs here that this Kellogg fellow may be our lunatic's next target?" the Captain pressed.

"It all adds up, Captain," Briggs said before she could respond.

"What all adds up?" asked Detective Hunter Whitloe, stepping through the Captain's office door.

"Hunter," Atherton said. "I think your partner, Briggs, here just solved our little killing spree."

Jonathan Briggs looked squarely at the detective, grinning ear to ear. For the first time in a long while, Whitloe didn't know what to say.

***

"It helps if you don't look," the burly black woman in hospital whites said to me after tightening the tourniquet on my arm and patting the inside of my elbow for a vein.

I turned my head slightly to the right but still could see as she prepared the needle for my blood test. I clenched my fist. I hated this.

"And relax," she said. "This won't hurt a bit."

Why do they always say that? I wondered. Then the prick came.

"Unclench your fist," she said, "and relax."

I couldn't fucking relax. I had just spent a good forty-five minutes watching a required HIV/AIDS informational video, and damn if I didn't recognize one of the speakers in it. His name was Kevin, and he was someone I had met casually — through a friend in a bar in San Francisco — when I first moved to California after undergraduate school in Virginia in 1986. His gaunt features stared at me, and he listed the known and possible ways to contract HIV, with a subtitle that read: KEVIN — LIVING WITH AIDS, underneath him.

"Tell me why you've come to get tested," a female counselor more than twice my age had asked when I first walked in and took a seat in her cubicle about an hour ago.

"Well," I fumbled, "I'm in a high-risk group."

"What do you mean, 'high-risk group'?" she asked. "I ask because many people who say that don't really understand what that term means. Are you an IV-drug user, for instance?"

"No," I said. "I'm *Haitian.*"

She paused for a minute, then said, "Haitians are no longer considered. . ."

"I know. I was trying to be funny. Bad joke. I suppose I'm just nervous." It was my turn to pause. "I'm gay."

She looked like I had just slapped her in the face, and I could tell that until this moment she never expected *that* response. I guess I never did fit middle-America's stereotype of the limp-wristed, lisping queen, and even though this would hardly qualify as "middle-America," I too often found similarities in the thinking there and the thinking here, only thirty miles east of San Francisco.

"I see," she said simply. "Well, you know that *homosexuals* are. . ."

"'Gay,'" I repeated, countering her condescension with a forceful tone. "And to be honest, I've been through all of this before. I get tested every six months."

"Well, good for you," she said, although I could tell she didn't mean it. She forced a handful of leaflets at me, complete with a condom and test-size sample of water-based lubricant, and said, "Just take this number over to the lab, and wait to be called."

I could tell she was getting very uncomfortable because she forgot to schedule the follow-up visit for my results. I reminded her.

"So that'll be on Tuesday, March 9th, at 4:30 pm," she said, scribbling a written reminder, then handing that to me as well. "Good day."

"Now, that wasn't bad, was it?" asked the black nurse with the needle, jarring me back to the present. I saw her put my numbered label on the blood vial.

"No," I said. "Thanks for putting up with me. I guess I'm just a big baby when it comes to needles."

"You were just fine, sir. You have a nice day, now, you hear?"

"Thanks again," I said, but as I left I had to wonder if she would have been as friendly if I had told *her* that I was gay.

***

Hunter Whitloe tried to re-cap the last hour's discussion with the Captain, Briggs, and Burton. Samuels had come in about half-way through.

"So, you do agree, Captain, that we should provide this Artie Kellogg with some sort of police protection?" he asked. He looked at the flier to be sure he had the kid's name right.

"I think it would be in the best interest of all concerned," Deputy Samuels piped in before Atherton responded.

"And I'll handle it personally, sir," Whitloe said. "I can set up in an adjoining room at the kid's hotel, and. . ."

"This is Briggs's brainstorm, Hunter," the Captain said.

"Wow, a stakeout," Briggs breathed.

Whitloe tried not to explode. "With all due respect, sir. . ."

"Stop saying that, Hunter. We know you don't mean it. What's your point?"

The detective cleared his throat and cast a glance toward his junior officer, the fuck-up. "Sir, I *am* the senior officer on this case, and while we all appreciate Deputy Briggs's insight here, I'm sure we all would agree that as senior officer, and the head of Special Investigations, I should. . ."

"Very well, Hunter," Atherton said. "I see your point, however self-serving it may be. And I'll allow you to do this. . ."

"Thank you, sir," Whitloe interrupted.

"*If* you take Deputy Briggs along as your back-up," he finished.

"But, sir. . ."

With no pride to bruise, Jonathan Briggs started to speak. "Captain, Birdie and I still have quite a few postal machines to check out. It may take the better part of Thursday and, maybe, Friday, so I don't know how effective I would be if I went along with the Lieutenant."

"That's right," Whitloe said. "And we'll need someone here to coordinate the increased security we're sending to the high school on Friday. Briggs can man the station and act as home base." He looked at the other deputy. "We can put Samuels on-site at Marshall Clancy Friday morning until I arrive with this Kellogg fellow."

"That's fine with me," the Captain said. "Is it okay with you, Briggs?"

"No problem," Briggs replied.

Hunter tried not to fume at this point.

"Well, Hunter," Atherton said, "we'll run it your way. Check in at the Sheraton immediately, and start your around-the-clock surveillance. I want you to radio in *anything* that seems odd or out of the ordinary. Briggs, you and Burton follow through on your postal label machine search, but be back here at 0600 Friday morning to oversee things on this end for Friday's little assembly. Samuels, set up an appropriate security team for the high school, and be sure to clear it all with the Marshall Clancy principal. But keep it low key. I don't want anything too suspicious. We don't need everyone and their mother asking questions. Understand?"

"Yes, sir," Samuels said.

"Very well. You've all got your work cut out for you. Get moving."

Samuels was first out, followed by Briggs and Burton. As Whitloe turned to head out the door, Atherton said, "Hunter, you've got a good team there. *Use them.*"

"Yes, sir," Whitloe mumbled quietly. A few minutes later, he was on the phone to his wife to tell her he wouldn't be home until Friday.

***

I got home some time after five-thirty and walked the dog before I listened to my answering machine. First came Otto's message from last night, telling me of Terry Totah's demise; second was a quick clip from Pamela, thanking me for a nice evening out.

"*Let's do it again some time,*" the machine played back her voice. "*Oh, speaking about doing it again, you never did tell me when I can expect to see your name in the paper under some huge headline. I'll keep my eyes peeled. Bye.*"

My mind instantly recalled my mid-morning "discussion" with Charlotte Journigan, and I found myself wondering the same thing Pamela had. I reached for the bandage in the crook of my left elbow and pulled it off, yanking a number of hairs along with it.

BEEP.

"*Paul, it's Davin. Haven't heard from you in a couple of weeks and was wondering—if you aren't doing anything tonight—if you'd like to meet me and a few friends at the club for a drink. It'd be nice to see you. Hope you can make it.*"

The answering machine tape ended, and I caught myself smiling for what had to be the first time today.

After an hour-and-a-half workout on my weight bench and a light dinner of pasta in a vinaigrette, I took a quick shower and readied myself for an evening at Chestnut Grove's gay bar, The Crystal Ball. Tuesdays drew the country-and-western crowd, and I stared in my closet long and hard before coming up with suitable attire. My tastes in scenes and music never really drifted toward country, but I managed to find a passable outfit in a pair of black jeans, brown steel-toed boots, and a red and black checked flannel shirt with T-shirt underneath. My only bolo had been a skull-and-crossbones given to me by Pamela as a joke, so I decided to leave it at home. Maybe, if I dropped the right hints, I could land a black Stetson from her for my birthday.

I pulled my Jeep into the parking lot of the town's 7-Eleven after eight o'clock. The bar shared the back half of the building, with a single, secluded entrance around the side. As I approached, I could hear the strains of a Clint Black tune, topped by the voice of the evening's two-step instructor for the dance lessons that took place from seven to nine.

"Bud Light, Andy," I told the bartender when I made it inside and over to the long bar that dominated the wall across from the front door. I laid three dollar bills in front of me.

"Hey, Paul," he said. "Good to see you. It's been a while." He flashed a smile that had me lust after him ever since I had moved here, but I had a few rules for living, and *Never Sleep with a Bartender* was near the top of the list. Too much grist for the rumor mill, and murder on your reputation if your performance wasn't up to par.

"Thanks," I replied. "Actually, I'm here to meet Davin. Have you. . .?"

"Stop that man! I want to get off!" came a voice from behind.

"Hello, Ruby," I said without having to turn around. But turn around I did, extending my hand.

Chestnut Grove's legendary drag queen, Ruby Slippers, scoffed at the low-keyed gesture, throwing her arms out wide to embrace me fully. (Since Ruby had chosen to live life in costume, even going through the legal time and expense of a name change, everyone now referred to him as "her;" he, of course, was "she.") She had once told me she was here long before there ever was a bar called The Crystal Ball, and that she'd be around very long after, and I put her age somewhere in the late forties or early fifties, but I knew better than to ask. Besides, her meticulous make-up work covered any signs of aging, and her almost perfectly feminine appearance had frozen her — gracefully — at twenty-nine.

"Thank God you're finally here," she said, escorting me to a chest-high cocktail table surrounded by five other men. "You're a writer. I need a professional opinion."

"If I have one," I said. I sent a glance to those around the table, with a smile and a nod "hello."

"Oh my," Ruby said, interrupting her own thought. "Where are my manners? Paul, you do know everyone, don't you?"

"I think so," I replied, making a sweep. "Bo. . .Martin, nice to see you," I said with a half-salute to the two standing closest together. Martin was a dark-haired, clean-cut collegiate type, and his partner of three years, Bo, had blond hair that he had recently grown into a short pony tail. They had moved from Sacramento over a year ago, with their friend, Francisco, a younger Latino with a severe flattop and sideburns, who now stood next to them. Picking up an empty glass, Francisco readied to pour from a pitcher of beer.

"Mr. Blazer," he said, sliding a full glass over to the fourth, whom I did not know.

"I told you to cut that out," I said. Francisco had taken to calling me "Mr. Blazer" when he had learned I used to teach high school. It wasn't a respect thing; I think he wanted me to teach *him* something.

"This is Nolan," Ruby said of the fourth man. He wore a pair of wire-rimmed glasses beneath his rather red hair, and his smile was a testament to many years of dental work that eventually paid off. At what I guessed to be a little over six-feet, he was the tallest of the group.

"How are you, Paul? Glad you could make it," said the fifth.

"Davin," I said simply. I could tell I was blushing, and with the house lights up higher than normal for the dance lessons, I figured everyone else could notice, too. "Thanks for the call. It brightened my day."

"All right, enough of the social pleasantries," Ruby said. "As I said, we were deep in a very important literary discussion, and I would appreciate your input."

"Shoot," I said, sending a wink to Davin to tell him I'd continue our talk in a moment.

"Well, the fascinating news is that I've decided to write my autobiography," she said, "but I just can't decide on a title. I've narrowed it down to two." With the performance skill she had lived half her life to master, she spoke her pair of options dramatically. "*Like Pearls Before Swine*," she said, sweeping her left arm for effect. "Or, *The Sound of Piss on Porcelain*." Her right arm moved the other way. She paused for a moment, then asked, "What do you think?"

I said nothing for as long as I could, then Bo chimed in.

"I like the second," he said. "Imagine the drama it would evoke, and if there's one thing about you, Ruby, it's drama."

"True," she said.

"I have to agree with Bo," Francisco concurred.

"Nolan and I prefer *Like Pearls Before Swine*," noted Martin. "Don't we, Nolan?"

Nolan was caught in mid-swig, and he just nodded with frothy lips.

"What do you think, Davin?" I asked, hoping to delay my response further.

Throwing up his hands, he cried, "I'm staying out of this." With that, he headed toward the Men's Room.

"Paul?" Ruby said. "It's two to two. Your vote will decide it. What do you think?"

Clearing my throat, I answered. "You know, it's difficult to think with all of this twanging music, and maybe you can come up with something else to consider. How about, *You've Gotta Have Balls to Wear a Dress Like That*? You want something that really speaks to who you are, not some pretext about you, you know?"

"But I *am* everything I pretend to be," Ruby said, then she lit up. "Hey. Maybe that's it. *I'm Everything I Pretend to Be: The Undeniably Fabulous Life of Moi, Ruby Slippers*. I love it." She leaned over and planted a kiss firmly on my cheek. The lipstick smeared as she pulled away. "Paul, you're a genius!"

"Thanks," I said. "I *am* a writer, you know." Bringing a napkin to my face, I said, "Now, if you'll excuse me," and made my way to the restroom.

"Simply brilliant," I heard Nolan say as the Men's Room door closed.

"So," said Davin, "did you come up with something?"

"Maybe," I said. "But you know her better than anyone else. She'll probably change her mind a dozen times before she's finished writing, if she *is* writing, that is."

"I know what you mean." Davin had followed around in Ruby's shadow ever since I knew him, making his connections in the gay subculture through her introductions. I had met him through her, in fact, when she still referred to him as her "Lady in Waiting." But somehow I could tell that Davin was growing tired of that scene and yearned to strike out and discover who he really was. From where I stood, it was a very exciting position to be in, and I found myself admiring him for it. As I got closer to thirty, I often had to wonder if anything I had done in life really made a difference. What would I have done differently, if I could?

Maybe finally settle down with someone.

I thought of Scott, my ex, who was supposed to be "The One," but who instead skipped to Los Angeles when things got a little shaky. The one I thought I had let go, until I received his Christmas Card some four years later, telling me he's HIV-positive. Would I ever be able to move on?

What if I were infected, too?

"What are you thinking about?" Davin asked me as someone else in a large cowboy hat opened the door and came in. He walked to the urinal and unzipped.

The Sound of Piss on Porcelain, I thought. "You," I lied instead. "Thanks again for calling and dragging me out tonight. It's been a long day."

"No problem," he said. He dampened a papertowel from under the sink and gently rubbed off Ruby's lipstick traces. "Like I said, it's good to see you."

Maybe finally settling down with someone, I thought again. "You know," I said, struggling for the words, "I guess I wanted to say I'm sorry for not calling you as often as I should. I mean, we were going out pretty consistently for a while, then. . .I don't know. Maybe I got cold feet or something."

"Really," Davin said, "its okay."

I smiled, sensing that he understood.

"It's like I've heard you say, anyway. One of your Rules for Living, I think: *An ex is an ex for a reason.*" He opened the door. "So, what do you think of Nolan? Cute, huh."

I followed him back to our friends without a word and ordered another beer and a shot of tequila when Andy made his rounds. Looking at Andy then over to Davin, I wondered if it weren't about time to start breaking some of those rules.

***

By ten-thirty Wednesday morning, Hunter Whitloe had set up a working surveillance station in the room adjoining Artie Kellogg's at the Sheraton, complete with monitors for the two hidden cameras in the young man's room, a reel-to-reel recorder for the mic and telephone tap, and a motion sensor to tell him whenever the front door was opened. Deputy Samuels had come by about an hour earlier, dropping off a fax machine and a duffel bag of clothes that Gladys had insisted on packing for him. They had discussed Samuels's setting up the security team at Marshall Clancy High for Friday, and the deputy had left to make arrangements with the principal, Orin Brandriff.

Whitloe poured over the medical records of Terry Totah that Samuels had been able to obtain yesterday from the man's doctor. Totah had a history of high blood pressure and a slight heart murmur, and against his doctor's better judgment, he continued overdoing the aerobic activity and living with the stress of producing his cable access fitness program. On top of that, he was a chain smoker.

"Routine," he said, echoing the words of coroner Redford Malone. "Standard M.I." He looked over a few other pages. "Looks like you had it coming," he said. "Shit."

Matthew Black had become such a recluse in his last few years of life, he rarely saw his physician, and no immediate records were available when Hunter called for them. He hadn't been a smoker, though, to the best of his doctor's recollection, and Hunter didn't find any evidence of cigarette butts in the death scene photographs. Taggert finding high concentrations of nicotine in him still didn't make sense.

Unless he was on "The Patch", the detective thought suddenly. He picked up the phone and called the medical examiner's office.

"Medical Examiner's," came the voice through the phone. "Taggert here."

"Doc, it's Hunter. I just thought of something. What would happen to a non-smoker who wore the patch?"

"'The patch'?" she repeated. "You mean a trans-dermal nicotine patch, to *quit* smoking. Who the hell would do that?"

"Just play along with me for a minute," Whitloe said.

Taggert paused, then said, "He'd get a hell of a rush, like smoking a cigarette for the first time. Rapid heart beat, headache, perhaps. . ."

"But could it *kill* him?"

"Hunter, where are you going with this?"

"You said you found a high concentration of nicotine in Matthew Black, right?" he asked. "How did it get there? Nothing I have says he was a smoker."

"Maybe he *was* quitting, Hunter. You'd have to put a good number of those patches on you — for quite a while — to kill you. Not a very attractive form of suicide, I think."

"But what if. . .?"

"And not a very effective way to *murder* anyone. Would you sit there as some goofball covered you with little sticky patches? I don't think so. And wait a minute," she said. Whitloe could tell she had set down the receiver. A moment later, she returned. "I've got the Black report here,

Hunter, and thank you. Your little theory just helped solve one of my own mysteries."

"What's that?" the detective asked, deflating a little.

"Black came in with a small, red welt a few inches below his left nipple," she said. "I had ruled out burn or scar of some sort, but *Probable irritation from trans-dermal nicotine system patch*," she continued, in such a way Whitloe could tell she was writing as she spoke, "that about covers it. It also accounts for the nicotine we found. Brilliant, Detective. And thanks."

"Don't mention it," he said. "Just *one* red welt, huh?"

"Just one," she confirmed. "I'd have certainly found plenty more if this phantom killer of yours had somehow incapacitated the man and had covered him head to toe. Sorry, Hunter. Anything else?"

"Nah," he said. "I'll let you go. Bye." As he hung up, a knock sounded from the hotel room's adjoining door, startling him a bit. "What is it?"

"It's me, Detective Whitloe. . .Artie. I'm going to visit my girlfriend, and I thought I should let you know."

Hunter got up and opened the door, shouldering his .357 and slipping on a jacket to conceal it in the process. "Wait for me," he said.

The kid gave him a stare. "You're kidding, right? I mean, I know you're around to protect me, and all, but. . ."

"I'm with you like stink on shit until Friday, Mr. Kellogg. I'll wait in her living room or out in the car if you stay there. I'll be your chaperone if you decide to go out. I know this isn't pleasant for either of us, but believe me, it's for the best."

"Okay, man," he said, and he turned to leave through the front door. "Whatever. I just hope you're not, like, into watching people like that, or something."

Whitloe said nothing. Instead, he looked over to the surveillance console to be sure everything was on as they left. *This was going to be a long couple of days*, he thought.

"Thanks, Lieutenant," Artie Kellogg said at the end of the day, his tone heavy with sarcasm. "You're a wonderful man, and a very nice date, and I really can't wait until tomorrow to do it all over again." The kid faked a smile, and topping it off, he mockingly gave the detective a quick wink before sliding his key in the hotel room's door lock and going inside.

"Very funny," Whitloe said, opening his own door. "See you in the morning." He knew that Kellogg had been kidding, but he felt nauseated by their last exchange all the same. When inside his room, he briefly checked his equipment for any signs of activity while they had been away. Apart from the standard maid and turn-down service, there appeared to be none, so Whitloe changed into his pajama bottoms, turned out the light, and crawled under the stiff comforter for the night.

Again, he slept fitfully, if at all.

The Sheraton's breakfast chef struck a bell, summoning one of the hotel's new room service runners whom he hadn't seen before.

"Here," the chef said, pushing the usual continental breakfast fare — a glass of orange juice, two slices of toast, scrambled eggs, and some cereal — toward him. "This goes to a Mr. Kellogg," he explained, consulting the order ticket. "Room 203."

The server accepted the goods with a brief nod and placed them carefully on a room service cart. "Kellogg. Room 203. Got it," he said. Looking at the check, which he placed next to the small box of Trix on the table, he mumbled something to himself.

"Don't worry," the chef said. "The bill might be small, but they usually produce the biggest tips. You're up earlier than they are, you know." He returned to the griddle to check on a batch of waffles as the server wheeled away. "Where do they find these losers?" he said to himself.

The combination of a light knocking at Artie Kellogg's door along with the piercing sound of the motion sensor as the kid opened it early that Thursday morning jolted Hunter Whitloe off his bed and through the door that connected their two rooms. With the speed at which he moved and with the little light provided by a small lamp near Artie's bed, most of what happened next was a blur. All the detective could remember seeing clearly was the small, single-serving-sized box of Trix on the room service cart just before he tackled the gangly boy in white behind it.

"Jeez, Lieutenant," Kellogg said, recovering from the shove Whitloe had given him as he passed. "What's wrong with you? Haven't you ever ordered room service before?"

Whitloe lifted himself up a bit, staring first at the terrified face of the Sheraton's newest employee, then back at the kid he was supposed to be protecting.

"Room service?" he repeated. He got up with a hand still firmly holding onto the breakfast food runner. "Who the hell told you you could order room service?" He looked at the hotel employee. "Is that true? Do you work here?"

The young man in white stood with a little effort and said, "Not any more!" Throwing down the napkin he had draped over one arm, he stormed down the hallway. "And you can keep your fucking tip," he yelled back. "You tight wad!"

"I thought you might be hungry," Kellogg said. "I sure as hell was, so I called down for some food. I didn't think it'd be such a big deal."

Whitloe steadied himself to his feet and wheeled the cart inside. "What about this?" he asked, indicating the Trix.

"After what you told me yesterday, you know, why you're here, and all," he said, "I thought you'd find it funny. Apparently not."

"No," Whitloe confirmed angrily. "*Apparently not.*" Everyone's a fucking joker, he thought.

The rest of the morning passed without incident, and besides his almost unshakable feeling of embarrassment, Whitloe's only thought was: Briggs had been right. It would be Friday. Goddamn it, Briggs had been right.

***

"I'm running down to the mailroom," Otto Nicholson said to me that afternoon. "Need anything?" He carried a small basket of out-going mail he had collected from the desks in our department.

I opened my lap-level drawer and scanned my supplies. "Nope," I answered. "But if you go by the Coke machine, I'll have a Mr. Pibb." I fished through my pants pocket and retrieved three quarters.

He waved me on. "Okay, but it's on me. I'm feeling kind of thirsty myself."

Twenty minutes later, Otto returned with my soda and a Jolt cola for himself. "All the sugar. . .twice the caffeine," he said, reciting the drink's slogan. "I think it may be one of those kind of days." Popping the top, he took a long swig, then sat down at his desk behind me.

Not another one, I thought. Charlotte had effectively snubbed me since our talk two days ago, and I fought hard to look busy with my usual research for the incoming obituaries. I wasn't sure what it would take, but I definitely wanted some action.

"Oh my God. Help!" came the voice of Cindi Bates behind me.

I turned to see her running toward Otto's desk, and in that instant I knew something was wrong. I couldn't see Otto. He had disappeared. When I got up, however, I saw one of his legs extending from underneath his desk, with the rest of him flat on the floor. His cola lay beside him on its side, its contents puddling and expanding quickly.

"Otto, are you all right?" I asked. "What's the matter?" I lifted his head and cradled it in my arm. When I placed a hand on his chest, I could feel his heart pounding, and as I leaned closer to hear his reply, I noticed an odd, fruity smell to his breath. "Otto, are you okay? What's wrong?"

"Diabetic," he managed. "Coffee room fridge. . .insulin. . ."

"Go," I said to Cindi. My grandmother had been a diabetic, and seeing Otto like this, I realized that he was having an episode that required his medication.

By this time, a good half dozen people had gathered around us, including an uncharacteristically unnerved Charlotte Journigan. "Blazer, is he okay?"

Otto raised his hand and pulled at the handle of the lower drawer to his desk. "No feeling," he said as his hand refused to respond, dropping to the floor. I opened it for him, and there I found a single hypodermic needle.

"Here," Cindi Bates said, returning from the refrigerator with a styrofoam package marked, "INJECTABLE INSULIN — Keep Refrigerated."

"Let's give them some room, people," Charlotte said. She extended her arms to disburse the others. "Everything's going to be fine. Show's over. Back to work."

I took a glass bottle from the package, and with a small gesture, Otto showed me how far to fill the needle. "In the thigh," he said, and he struggled to unbuckle his pants.

Both Cindi Bates and Charlotte turned away in the interest of privacy, although I could see the Assistant News Editor turn her head toward us once to check on us. In half a minute, it was over, and I withdrew the hypodermic from Otto's leg. A few moments later, I had him sitting up against his desk.

"You had me worried there, my friend," I said. "I thought for a minute I'd be writing *your* obituary for tomorrow's paper."

"You're not getting my job that easily, Blazer," he replied. "I can usually keep this in check by watching my weight, exercising, and eating a sensible diet, whatever that is." He rested there for at least fifteen minutes as the insulin took effect. Shortly, his breathing went back to normal, and his pulse had slowed.

"Nicholson," Charlotte said, "you get home and rest. Blazer, can you take him?"

"No, no, no," Otto said before I could reply. He struggled to his chair. "No sense having both of us out. There's work to do, and see," he said, moving his fingers, "the numbness is going away. I'm feeling much better already, really. I can make it on my own, thank you."

"Otto. . ." I tried.

"Very well, then, you old fool," Charlotte interrupted. "Paul, there's never been any arguing with this man. I thought you knew that by now. You just be sure to wait this out for another fifteen minutes before you leave. Hear me?"

"I'll stop by tonight to check on you," I offered, feeling guilty. I had wished for some excitement around here, but not at this man's expense. "You can show me your aquarium."

Nicholson shook his head. "Call first, Paul. I may not be up for company." He put his syringe back in its case in his desk drawer after cleaning it. The bottle of insulin would be returned to the coffee room fridge on his way out. "Okay," I said. "You're sure you're steady enough to drive?"

"I've lived with this long enough to know when I'm fine and when I'm not, Paul. But thanks again for your concern. Despite my mood, it is greatly appreciated."

I watched as Otto took a bit longer than usual to stand, then he carefully gathered his things and teetered down the hallway toward home.

At the end of my work day, I drove my Jeep past Otto's address to see the borrowed company van parked in front of his house. Giving him the courtesy he had asked for, I decided to call him after dinner.

"*Wie geht's*, Dante?" I asked when I arrived home. "*Was tust du heute? Bist du hungrig*?" Although I doubted he'd respond to "How's everything?" and "What did you do today?" — my first two questions — I figured that *hungrig* would translate in almost any language. He marched over to his food dish, picked it up with his mouth, and brought it to me, understanding completely.

"*Sehr gut, mein Wunderhund.* Very Good." I filled his bowl from the 40-pound bag near the bathroom, and he ate happily, wagging his tail all the while.

MAYBE IF YOU WORKED OUT, EVERYTHING ELSE WILL, TOO, read a cross-stitched sign on the wall over my weight bench. It had been a gift from my mother when I last went back to Virginia to visit my parents. That was November 1991, after my six-month stint in jail for that murder I didn't commit. I had spent much of that time working out, as the days blended into weeks into months. She made such a fuss over how fit I had become that she and Dad started watching what they ate and began a weekly exercise routine, walking around the old neighborhood. Between workouts and her daytime soaps, she cross-stitched and presented me with her handiwork on the day I went home to Chestnut Grove to resume my life.

Figuring I had little more to lose that the low-grade depression that had been lingering on for the last few days, I decided to take my mother's advice. I changed into a pair of shorts and muscle-T and worked for an hour and forty-five minutes on my chest and back. Arms and shoulders would come tomorrow. Legs on Saturday, before the trip to the Star Trek convention in San Francisco with Otto.

After my workout, I walked the dog, took a shower, then tried Otto's number to see how he was fairing. The line rang busy for the better part of the evening, so I decided to give up and call it a night.

***

The Friday morning edition of the *Times* slammed against the screen door with a thud after bouncing off the welcome mat. A moment later, the wooden door behind it flew open, revealing a rather angry, middle aged man in flannel boxer shorts, his belly hanging over the waistband.

"What the hell is going on?" he bellowed. Staring down at the newspaper, he flashed three shades of red. "Goddammit, I thought I. . . HEY!" He saw movement at the end of his driveway and called, "Did you do this? Get your ass over here! I don't want this fucking rag delivered to my house, understand?" He picked up the paper and swung the screen door open. "Get inside while I call your boss again. I'll have your fucking job before this morning's out."

Closing the door, he threw the newspaper to the floor then crossed through his living room to make his telephone call. "I've been to Disneyland, you know. I know how to deal with Mickey Mouse organizations like yours. . ."

***

Deputy Jonathan Briggs manned the operations at the Chestnut Grove Police station at 0600 Friday, as Captain Atherton had ordered. By seven o'clock, he had received the "All Clear" from Samuels and the security team at Marshall Clancy High, and Lieutenant Whitloe had called in to say that he and the man-of-the-hour, Artie Kellogg, were on their way to the school.

He tried to put his recent set of disappointments in the back of his mind: his search for the postage labeling machine had produced little more than blisters on his and Birdie Burton's feet when they had reached the last store on their list at the end of yesterday afternoon. But the importance of that lead faded as the events of this morning unfolded. Today, they were going to catch a killer.

"So far, so good," Samuels said, greeting Whitloe as he stepped into the school's auditorium. Students would be filling in within a few hours, and the Kellogg kid was setting up in a dressing room behind the stage, under armed guard.

"Keeping the kid alive is one thing," Whitloe said. "But it's only half of what we're here for. I want this joker, and I want him bad."

Samuels pointed to a few of the places where he had laid out his officers. "We're pretty well covered, sir. No one's going to get in or out of here without getting noticed. The kids'll all be easy to spot, and I've got all the adults — teachers and staff — wearing distinctive name badges. He won't slip through."

"Good work," the detective said. "Now all we have to do is wait."

Pamela Lawson walked down English hall and caught sight of a uniformed police officer standing guard at the end of a row of lockers. As she rounded onto Math hall, she saw two more.

Getting to the phone in the faculty workroom, she dialed her friend, Paul Blazer, to see if he or the paper knew anything about this increase in police presence for what was to have been a routine all-school assembly. The phone rang twice before one of the officers opened the workroom door suddenly, startling her.

"Identification, miss," he said sternly.

And what's with these stupid nametags? she wondered, flashing hers.

"Thank you, ma'am," the officer said. "Sorry to have bothered you."

Pamela hung up the receiver before Paul picked up, and the man disappeared behind the faculty workroom door as it closed. She would call later.

"I have to tell you," Artie Kellogg toned into his microphone, on stage in front of half of the student body, "I didn't plan on having my life turning out this way, and I'm sure none of you expect this to happen to you. . ." His voice carried over a house of over six hundred, with nary a dry eye in the place.

"He's getting to them," Samuels said to Hunter Whitloe.

Whitloe yawned.

Then, the warble of the detective's cellular telephone cut through the sniffles around him until he brought the phone to his ear. "Whitloe here."

"Lieutenant," came the voice. Whitloe recognized it as that of his other deputy, and instantly became annoyed.

"What is it, Briggs? We're very busy here."

"I'm afraid we're a lot busier where we are, Lieutenant," Briggs said.

"What do you mean? Where are you?"

"We got a call about fifteen minutes ago," the deputy said. "We're at former councilman Nicholas Pirelli's, sir. He's dead."

Whitloe felt his insides sink. "Dead? How? Who found him?" A hundred questions ran through him at once, and he had to ask Briggs, of all people.

"Lucky Lucy did, sir."

To anyone else, this might have sounded like gibberish, but the detective knew "Lucky Lucy." He had to run her off a number of corners in the town when he caught her soliciting. He'd assumed she had turned over a new leaf since he hadn't seen her around in a while. Pirelli must have been another one of her customers. The girl was still turning. . .

"*Tricks*," Whitloe said aloud.

"We've got that, too, sir," Briggs responded. "We found him in the bedroom, and that cereal's all over the place."

"*Trix*," Whitloe said as it fell into place.

"You said that, Lieutenant. I heard you. Can you hear *me*? Do we have a bad connection, or something?"

"Never mind, Briggs. Don't touch anything. I'm on my way." Whitloe returned the cel phone to his belt and glared at Samuels. "A fucking wild goose chase," he said. "Councilman Pirelli bought it in his home across town."

"*Former* Councilman Pirelli," Samuels corrected him. "He was recalled, remember, after the town found him sleeping around with prostitutes. Big article in the paper, and. . ."

"Shut up, Samuels," the detective said. "Make sure all this gets cleaned up, and file your report. I've got some more cereal to step in."

Chapter Six

Two Scoops

THE FORMER — AND NOW "late" — Chestnut Grove city councilman, Nicholas Pirelli, lay propped up in his king-sized bed amid a set of rumpled silk sheets, an expensive down comforter, and about sixteen ounces of dry Trix cereal. Across his lap spanned a short-legged breakfast tray, the kind usually reserved for an intimate early morning in bed. The tray held an overturned glass of orange juice, a soft-boiled egg in a porcelain holder, and a large cereal bowl that had been filled past capacity. A spoon had been slipped into his right hand, now at his side, and a yellow linen napkin had one end draped over his bare chest and the other stuffed into his mouth.

"Suicide, Briggs?" Hunter Whitloe asked his partner as he surveyed the scene at a distance, from the bedroom door. Given the state of the last two bodies, the detective half expected to find this one in or at least near the kitchen. When he entered Pirelli's home, however, and wasn't instantly greeted with the sound of crunching cereal beneath his shoes, he almost wondered if Briggs had staged some elaborate joke in retaliation for the way he'd been treating him recently. That thought passed quickly when the deputy had called for him down the hallway.

"I don't think so, sir," Briggs said in all seriousness. "That napkin's a good indication he hadn't planned having his breakfast in bed. Not like this anyway."

Whitloe ignored the urge to say something smart. He carefully made his way toward the body, but even from a distance, he had noticed Pirelli's cheeks were full behind that cloth, and a mixture of milk and cereal had seeped through the corners of his mouth and down his chin.

This joker is twisted, the detective thought.

"I'll get the evidence kit and camera from the car," Briggs offered.

"You do that," Whitloe said.

Probation Officer Birdie Burton slid past Briggs as he moved back down the hall. "I've got the woman's statement, Lieutenant, you know, the one who found him. Should I let her go?"

The detective shot her a look. "Hell, no. Not until I've had a chance to talk to her. What are you doing here anyway? This is a little out of your jurisdiction, isn't it?"

Burton snorted. "There was no one else down at the station when we got the call," she said. "Every available officer had been dispatched to *your* location for that dead-end you walked into this morning."

"A dead-end that your boyfriend there set up for us," Whitloe spat back, unable to control his temper. "None of this would have happened if your little brainstorming session with the boy wonder hadn't sent all of us scrambling in the wrong direction."

"Don't try to blame this on me. . .or him! We *all* agreed that Kellogg was a very likely target. It made more sense than this bozo," she said, with an outstretched finger toward Pirelli.

Whitloe wasn't about to explain the hooker connection to all of this, but what she said did make him think. Everything *had* pointed to Kellogg, but it could just have easily meant the former councilman was the next victim. Some other piece was still missing, and he could do nothing but wonder what it was.

"Look, Burton," he said. "I didn't mean to blow up at you like that."

"Save it, Lieutenant," she fumed. "I'll be out here in the living room with Lucky Lucy. I'll try to prepare her for the pleasure of speaking with you."

Jonathan Briggs came back with his camera bag over his shoulder and the evidence kit in hand. "What was that about?"

Whitloe moved past him and said, "Start taking pictures, Briggs, but don't touch anything."

"Gotcha," the deputy said. He fished his Nikon out, twisted on a wide-angle lens and a flash attachment, and began to shoot.

"Lucy," Whitloe said when he entered the living room. "I need to ask you some questions." He looked at the probation officer. "Briggs says you're a pretty good sketch artist," he improvised as an unspoken apology. "Why don't you go back there, and draw a few things for me. And. . ."

"'Don't touch anything,'" she said with a slight smile. "Okay, Lieutenant." She handed him her notes containing Lucky Lucy's statement.

"Thanks," he said, reading it. With his eyes trained on the paper, though, he tripped over the rubber-banded edition of the *Times* Pirelli had brought into his living room. "What the. . .?" He turned toward the retreating form of Birdie Burton. "Get me a pair of rubber gloves from the evidence kit," he called to her. Reaching for his cellular phone at his hip, he dialed the station.

"Chestnut Grove Police Sta. . ."

"It's Whitloe. Has Deputy Samuels made it back yet?"

"Why, yes sir," the voice said. "He's just coming in the. . ." The phone changed hands.

"Samuels here."

"Look through my files on the Black and Totah cases, and tell me the name of the paper boy for those areas," Whitloe said.

"Sir?"

"Just do it!"

After a pause, Samuels came back to say, "There's no note of it in the Totah file, sir, but here in Matthew Black's you've got written an 'Antonio Tyger.' You spoke to him regarding the note Mr. Black had left for him about his service, dated 2/19. Last Friday."

All the running around he had been doing for the Artie Kellogg debacle had prevented him from following through on his newspaper carrier lead. That might be the missing piece to this, he thought.

"Get your butt down to the *Times*," he said, "and find out who the carrier is for Totah's neighborhood and for Nicholas Pirelli. If anyone gives you any lip, tell them you'll arrest them for interfering with an official investigation if they don't cooperate. Don't leak anything about this Pirelli thing. Just get me the kid's name and address."

And I'll bet a week's pay that it's that Antonio Tyger fellow, he thought. *And I'll be fucked if he goes by the name "Tony."*

***

The phone on my desk rang shortly before ten, and I was a little surprised to recognize Pamela Lawson's voice on the other end when I answered it.

"What's up, Pamela?" I asked. "Playing hooky?"

"Now isn't the time for your little jokes, Paul. I've spent the better part of the morning surrounded by the police."

"Pol. . ."

"That's right. The police. This place has been swarming with them since seven o'clock this morning, just before Artie Kellogg arrived for our school assembly."

My mind tried to sort through all she was saying. It was still stuck on "the police." "So, you're at the school," I said slowly.

"You'd think the kid was the President or something," she said. "And all the faculty and staff had to be cleared ahead of time, and we had to wear these stupid name badges. Paul, what's going on?"

"How would I know?" I was now more confused than ever.

"Come on," she said. "You work for a *newspaper*. Why would more than half of the city's police force show up at a high school for some kid talking about DUI? It doesn't make sense."

"No, it doesn't," I replied. Looking up from my desk, I saw Charlotte Journigan escorting a beige-clad officer of the law into her office rather quickly, closing the door behind her. "And neither does that."

"What?" Pamela asked.

My voice fell to a whisper. "The Assistant News Editor just got a visit from one of Chestnut Grove's finest. She's in her office with him right now."

"You've got to find out what's going on, Paul. This is too weird."

"You can say that again," I said. "I'll see what I can do."

"Can I get you something from the drink machine, Paul?" Otto Nicholson asked as I hung up the phone.

"Otto," I said, trying not to sound distracted. "How are you feeling?"

"Much better, thanks. My doctor says I need to watch my sugar intake more closely."

"Lay off the Jolt cola, will you?"

Otto raised a tall plastic bottle of Evian and said, "I'm covered. How about you?"

"No thanks," I said. I looked back to Charlotte's office. The door was still closed. "I'm fine for now."

"Suit yourself," he said. He returned to his work, and a moment later I could hear him whistling faintly. He was back to his old self.

I just wish I were.

"Everything okay, Chief?" I asked, poking my head into Charlotte's office half an hour later, after the policeman had left.

"Don't call me 'Chief'!" she said, a bit on edge. "Everything's fine." She struck a Camel and puffed away, turning in her swivel chair to look out her window. "Don't you have something to do, Blazer?"

"Uh. . ."

"If not," she said, "I can have you alphabetize some back-issue research or file something extremely tedious."

"That won't be necessary," I said quickly. "Sorry to have bothered you."

Backing my way out of her office and closing the door, I nearly bumped into a young woman who had stepped up behind me. "Pardon me," I said.

She looked at me through a rather frightened expression and said, "Maybe you can help me." She grabbed my arm and pulled me away from Charlotte's door.

"If you need an editor, or a reporter, I can get someone for you," I said. "If you want classifieds, they're down the hall." I pointed.

"No," she said. "I need to talk to someone who can watch out for me if they have to." Giving me the once over, she continued, "And from the looks of it, you're just about the only one around here who qualifies."

"I don't understand."

She whispered, "I need to tell you about a murder."

It was this that had me take a good look at her for the first time. She wore a black negligee under a brown trench coat, her bare legs ending in a pair of stiletto heels. Her hair was beyond windblown, and her make-up had smeared and run. She looked as if she had been crying.

Homeless, I thought.

Or crazy. Probably *both.*

Now, I grabbed her arm to usher her to the front door. "It sounds like you should be talking with the police," I said softly, trying to avoid a scene.

"I've already done that," she said. "All morning, in fact. They're no help at all."

That seems to be the popular consensus, I thought, remembering my call with Pamela. "Maybe you should talk to someone in the News bureau," I offered.

"I want you," she said. "Or I'm taking this thing to *Hard Copy.*"

"I'm taking a break," I called over to Otto. "I'll be back in fifteen." I had led the woman outside under a small group of trees near the building before I took pause to question my sanity. "My name's Paul," I said. "What's yours?"

"My friends call me 'Lucky Lucy,'" she replied.

***

Coroner Tess "Toe Tag" Taggert arrived at Pirelli's house with two assistants and an ambulance shortly after Whitloe had dismissed the councilman's lady caller.

"So, what do you make of this?" the detective asked. "Another coincidence?"

Taggert stretched on a pair of rubber gloves and walked over to the bed. "You've tried for fingerprints, I guess," she said, ignoring him. She leaned over the deceased and paused, waiting for Whitloe's yes or no.

"Silver plate won't work," Whitloe said. "The guy's too hairy. We're hoping for some luck with the things on the breakfast tray and spoon." Those had been removed and set near the wall after Briggs had finished with his pictures.

Taggert withdrew a long thermometer from her coroner's bag. It confirmed the room temperature she had noted on the house's thermostat on her way in: 72°. Turning the body over, she inserted the rod, and after a few minutes, had a reading on Pirelli.

91.1°.

"The body cools at somewhere between one and two degrees an hour," she explained as she rolled him back over. "Given a normal body temperature, I'd say he died about five or six hours ago." She glanced at her watch. "Around five or six this morning." With her gloved hands, she raised the lids of his eyes, first the right one, then the left. "Any earlier, and his corneas would have clouded by now. His eyes are still rather clear.

"Early rig in the neck and jaw," she continued, feeling. "Lividity isn't fixed." Whitloe followed her direction to the purplish discoloration of the underside of the body, where the blood had begun to pool. "But pressure against the darkened skin doesn't blanch." She demonstrated this too. "He's dead all right." With her thumb and middle finger, she cocked back and gave Nicholas Pirelli a sound thump to the head, just as she always did with fresh corpses. She liked the hollow thud it produced. "And ripe, too." She gave a little laugh, both at her own levity in this situation and to the indignity of death in general, especially the way in which the former councilman had met it.

Whitloe walked over to the breakfast tray and crouched down. With gloved hands, he slid each item into an evidence bag, marking each tag as he went. First the egg, then its holder. The contents of the cereal bowl he tipped into a screw-topped jar, and the bowl itself he set aside to air dry before he would try for prints.

"Wait a minute," he said, moving to the glass of orange juice. "If they're being poisoned, maybe it's in here."

Taggert had heard him and replied, "There was nothing in the Black and Totah samples, Hunter. And there's an easy way to see if he actually drank the stuff. Give me a collection tray."

Hunter stood and handed her an oblong device that she rested just beneath Pirelli's chin. "On three, you remove the napkin," she instructed. "One. . .two. . .three."

Pirelli's mouth remained open, and its contents spilled into the oblong tray. With gloved finger, Taggert swabbed the inside to get any of the remaining stuff. Together, they examined the mixture of chewed Trix cereal and milk.

"No O.J. as far as I can tell," she said.

Whitloe poured the contents into an evidence container all the same. "You have to agree," he said, "that this one doesn't look like 'natural causes.'"

"You're right about that."

"This whole breakfast set-up has to be some elaborate prop, everything from the hard-boiled egg, to the juice, to the cereal. We even had toast at the Totah scene. This guy's really sick."

"And methodical," she added. "With a warped sense of humor. I like him."

Taggert's two assistants wheeled a stretcher down the hall but had to enter the bedroom without it when it wouldn't fit through the door.

"You are through with this, aren't you?" she asked Hunter, meaning the body.

"Take it," Whitloe said, and they did.

"Black, Totah, and now Pirelli," Taggert said. "All with times of death in the early morning hours, between five and six o'clock. All with the appearance that they'd been eating breakfast. All gagged with some kind of cereal. Who could be doing this? And why?"

Whitloe decided not to tell Taggert about the sample boxes of cereal he had been receiving shortly before the murders, or the fact that they all were — in all probability — on the same paper boy's early morning route. "I'm not sure," he said, "but a closer look at all three bodies could help."

"Malone and I'll get on it," she said, and with that, she walked out the door.

***

As I spoke with the woman who called herself "Lucky Lucy," I found myself taking leave of my senses with everything I said or thought.

"It was Councilman Pirelli. I found him gagged and murdered," she said.

A prominent city official killed, and I'm the only one who knows about it, I thought. *What a break; what a story*. Never mind that I could hardly shit without a certain Assistant News Editor finding out about it, and I wasn't on the top of her list at the moment.

"And there was all this fucking cereal everywhere," she said. "*Trix*."

Cereal? I thought, recalling how Matthew Black had died. *Could they both have been murdered? If there were some connection, and I were to expose it. . .* Forget that another small step out of line could very well cost me my job.

"Trix," she repeated. "I'm a call girl. Don't you get it? I could be next!"

"Here," I found myself saying. I had taken the key to my apartment off my key ring and was handing it to her. "I won't let anything happen to you. You can stay at my place until we figure this out."

Lucky Lucy stopped shaking a little.

"I live at 429 Cedarbrook Crescent," I said. "It's the in-law unit to the side. Separate entrance. You wait there until I get home around five." My mind made no mention of the danger I'd probably be in if she was, in fact, next on a killer's hit list.

"Thank you," she said softly. She took the key.

"Just remember to say 'Gesundheit' when you walk in," I remembered. "I have a dog."

Lucy gave me a puzzled look before turning and leaving for my home.

What the fuck are you doing? my brain screamed as I walked into the office. Panic immediately set in, and I wondered how I could take back the last fifteen minutes. My worry intensified as I looked around to see the news room now in total chaos.

"Henderson!" Charlotte Journigan called to a reporter nearest her, "take a photographer down to that son-of-a-bitch's house, and bring me back something for Page One. Jake, call down to paste-up, and have 'em leave me some space. We'll need it. Anita, haul ass downtown, and find a cop who *is* talking about this. I don't care what you have to do or say, just do it." Her voice dropped a little for her next comment, which I guess wasn't for everyone. "'Interfering with an official investigation,' my left tit," she said. "Fargnoli. . ."

"What's going on?" I asked Otto in a whisper, moving to his desk.

"From what I understand," he replied, "former councilman Nicholas Pirelli has been found dead this morning."

"What do we know so far?" I asked. I wondered how long it would be before a more seasoned reporter scooped my Big Break from me.

"Not much," Otto said. "Word came up from the news desk a few moments ago, but the police aren't willing to confirm it, even though our source is our emergency band scanner we've got downstairs."

"So, she suspects foul play?"

"I'd guess so, but she's being stonewalled. She can't get any details, and no one can locate the person who called it in."

"Keep me posted," I said, and I turned for the front door.

"I got the obituary assignment," he said. "You want some of the research?"

"Did she ask you to have me do it?"

"Well. . .not exactly."

"Then, no. I've got some other things to do anyway."

Otto got up and followed me to ask something else. "We're still on for the Con tomorrow, aren't we?"

"Wouldn't miss it," I assured him. "I'll come by around eight to get dressed. I'll bring my ears."

"See you then," he called to me just before I stepped outside.

"Gesundheit, doggie. Gesundheit. Good boy."

I opened the door to my apartment to find Lucky Lucy sitting just two feet inside, against the wall. Dante squatted about four feet away, cocking his head when she spoke, wanting to get closer to this stranger.

"You didn't tell me he was bigger than my car and could eat me for lunch," Lucy said, getting up.

The dog padded over for a sniff, and she withdrew her hand sharply.

"He's harmless." I said. "Really." I reached down and gave him a good scratch.

"I don't care," she said. "Thank God you're home early. I don't think I could have made it 'til five sitting on the floor like that."

Indicating a chair, I said, "You could have made yourself more comfortable. He wouldn't have bothered you."

Lucy took the seat. "Did you find out anything more about Councilman Pirelli?" she asked.

"Not much." I took a cassette recorder out of my dresser drawer and hit the "ON" and "PLAY/RECORD" buttons. "But I do have a lot more questions to ask you."

***

Figuring he had to wait until the high-school-aged Antonio Tyger got home from school, Deputy Samuels went to the newspaper carrier's home around three-thirty. He brushed off his beige uniform as he walked up the driveway and checked his gun in the holster at his side.

"Chestnut Grove Police Department," he said, knocking on the front door. "Is anybody home?"

No answer came, and half a minute later, Samuels pounded again.

"Police Department. Open up."

He got up on his toes to peer into the fanned glass across the top of the door. It was dark inside, but he thought he saw someone move. His next move came too slowly.

Two rifle blasts shot through the heavy wood, sending the deputy backward and falling down the front steps. He felt the warmth of his own blood as it spread across his chest, and he could hear the sound of a screen door slamming at the back of the house as his vision faded to black.

On the other side of town at the Chestnut Grove police station, Lieutenant Detective Hunter Whitloe came in from an afternoon down at the Criminalistics Lab in Martinez, dropping off the evidence he had collected from the Pirelli crime scene. It took a little work, but Whitloe was able to persuade an overworked Sydney Pincus to cross-check any results from this case with those from Black's and Totah's. He quietly prayed for a break in this whole thing.

And soon.

As he approached his desk, his eyes focused on the small 3" x 4" x 1-1/2" brown-wrapped package sitting in the middle of his blotter like some small prized statue in an Indiana Jones movie. Following the thought, he half expected a large, round boulder to come crashing through the ceiling, rolling toward him when he picked it up.

"Golden Grahams," he said, carefully opening it. "Golden *fucking* Grahams."

"Another one, Lieutenant?" It was Briggs.

"Leave me alone, Briggs," the frazzled detective snapped back. Sitting down, he rubbed a hand over his forehead.

"You know," the deputy said, "that makes four. I think it's more than a coincidence."

"Oh, do you now?"

"I mean aside from the obvious," Briggs explained. "Have you noticed that all of the cereals are made by *General Mills*? All of them. Wheaties. . .Total. . .Trix. . .and now, Golden Grahams."

Again, the rookie was right, Whitloe thought. Lame, but right.

"So what do you make of that, Einstein?" the detective asked.

"Did you know that there's some trouble brewing at General Mills?" Briggs said. "A lot of people raising a fuss over pesticides being sprayed over the grains in the fields. Could be a disgruntled worker or consumer or someone like that."

Come to think of it, Whitloe had seen something on the NBC Nightly News about that, but, jeez, what a nightmare that would be. Where was the Chestnut Grove angle? If they couldn't narrow it down to the local level, following up on it could take...

"Forever," Whitloe said aloud. Just then, he had a thought that would keep his bothersome little deputy out of his way for quite a long time. "Briggs," he said, "I think you may have something there. I want you to start with the distribution points in the Bay Area that move General Mills products to all the stores to see who had been buying these different cereals in the past few weeks. The big boxes as well as the multi-packs of these little ones. Then, move on that 'disgruntled employee' theory of yours. I like it."

"Lieutenant, that could take. . ."

"Forever," Whitloe said again. "You can take that probation officer girlfriend of yours if you have to. There's more than enough work for the both of you."

"Yes, sir," Briggs said, almost sorry he had brought it up.

"Lieutenant!" called the afternoon dispatcher. "Lieutenant! We've got an officer down in the south side. I think it's Samuels."

"Shit," Whitloe said. He bolted from his chair. "Where is he, Shirl?"

"They're taking him to Mercy General, sir. He's been shot."

"I'm on my way," he said. "Briggs, get started on your assignment."

Moments later, Whitloe ran through the doors to emergency at Mercy Hospital, nearly colliding with two orderlies and a woman in a wheelchair. "A police officer," he panted. "Gun shot wound. . .just a few minutes ago. . ."

One of the orderlies pointed to Admitting.

"I'm looking for a Deputy Samuels," he said, thinking, *Shit, I don't even remember his first name*. "He came in with a gun shot wound, I think. Not too long ago."

The nurse scanned her roster of recent arrivals. "Samuels, yes. . .he's been taken into surgery. I'm afraid it may be a while. You might want to have a seat."

Whitloe backed away, feeling a little lost. Not only could he not recall his deputy's first name, he didn't know if he had any next of kin.

***

When I could tell Lucy was growing tired of my questions, I turned the recorder off, but by then, she had told me plenty.

Pirelli had called her "service" early that morning, and she had been dispatched to his home around eight o'clock. When she arrived and found the man dead in his bedroom, force-fed a final meal of Trix cereal, she phoned the police. They had asked her the standard series of questions, which she dutifully relayed to me, then was sent on her way with a warning not to speak to anyone about what she had seen.

When I asked if she had ever met Pirelli before, she informed me that he was a regular. In fact, his penchant for ladies of the evening had been the center of the controversy that eventually had him removed from office.

When the scandal made the papers three years ago, a recall order ensued, and the man had to leave the political arena in disgrace.

I made a note to be sure to check the back issues of the *Times* for the complete set of details.

"You don't expect me to *share* that thing with you, do you?" Lucky Lucy asked, having looked around my one-room apartment and spying my full-size futon in the corner.

"We've got to keep you out of sight for now," I explained. "I can sleep on the floor."

As if on cue, Dante walked over to the mattress, hopped up, and lay down on it. He kicked out his hind legs to be sure to take up as much room as possible.

"Oh, no," she said. "I don't think so." Getting up, she walked around and asked, "Where's the rest of this place?"

Just then the phone rang.

"Hello," I said, answering it on the first ring.

"Paul, darling, it's Ruby. I'm right in the middle of this chapter of my autobiography, which I must say is going *fabulously*, and I'm stuck. I was calling for some advice from a professional writer."

"Ruby, now's really not a good time," I said. Lucy stared back at me impatiently.

"Oh," the drag queen said. "You're *entertaining*. I understand. I'll just. . ."

"It's not that. I do have someone here, but it's not a date. She's more of an informant, for an article I'm working on."

"*She*? Oh, I see," Ruby said. "Definitely not a date, then. But an *informant?* Oh, the intrigue."

I rolled my eyes and turned away from Lucky Lucy. "It's not that exciting, really. She's just in a little trouble, and I'm letting her stay here until it blows over."

"In your tiny villa? You've got to be joking."

"Afraid not."

"Look, I have plenty of space in my flat. Why don't you have her spend the time here? I'm sure she'd be far more comfortable, as would you, poor thing."

I tried to picture the two of them together until I remembered that Lucy had stumbled on a *murder*. "I couldn't let you do that, Ruby. It could be quite dangerous."

"All the more reason to bring her here," she countered. "Could you imagine the excitement it would add to my book? I could title the chapter something like, *I Hid a Fugitive from the Chain Gang*. What an idea. You simply must let her stay with me."

I mulled the option over for a few moments then conceded. "I'll check with her," I said, but could tell that Lucy had understood our conversation from my half of it because she was nodding wholeheartedly already. "We'll be over about seven, after dinner."

"Heavens, no," Ruby said. "Don't eat. We can all dine together over here. Then, how about a relaxing evening at The Crystal Ball for a cocktail or two?"

"Dinner sounds fine," I said, "but we'll decide what to do afterwards later."

"Suit yourself," Ruby said. "Ta."

Hanging up, I turned back to Lucy and said, "Well, we've found you other arrangements. I just hope you're up for it."

***

With a slight poke to the shoulder, a doctor woke Hunter Whitloe from a fitful snooze on a waiting room couch.

"Lieutenant? I'm Doctor Cavallo. Your friend, Mr. Samuels, has made it out of surgery and is resting in Intensive Care."

Whitloe rubbed his eyes. "How is he? Can I see him?"

"I'm afraid not, Lieutenant. Not just yet, anyway. His condition is stable, but he's under heavy sedation. Maybe in the morning. . ."

The detective got up. "What time is it?"

"After nine. You should go home and try again in the morning."

"Thanks, doc," he said. "Let him know I was by."

"Of course."

***

Lucy's introduction to Ruby Slippers went far smoother than I had anticipated. In fact, they seemed to hit it off almost immediately. After a four-course meal my friend had elaborately prepared, the two of them retreated to Ruby's bedroom to try on some of her dresses and exchange make-up tips.

"So, you think you'll be comfortable here?" I asked Lucy, poking my head into our host's bedroom.

"Now, don't you worry your pretty little head, Paul," Ruby said. "We'll be just fine."

Lucy passed me a look that concurred with what Ruby had said.

"I think we're going to be up for a while," Ruby continued. "Why don't you run along to the club without us. We may join you later."

"Okay," I said. "Have fun. And if anything comes up in the next few days, don't hesitate to call me."

"Sure, love. T.T.F.N.," the drag queen said. She handed a wig to her new-found friend. "Ta Ta For Now."

"Thanks for everything, Paul," Lucy said, leaning over to give me a small peck on the cheek. "You watch your back, too. I wouldn't want anything to happen to my knight in shining armor."

"Watch it, girlie," Ruby said playfully. "I saw him first. He's mine."

At The Crystal Ball, I waited in a short line to pay the Friday night cover charge, then ordered a Bud Light from Andy. A flurry of colored lights rounded the dance floor, and for it being rather early for a bar, the crowd was picking up quickly.

I chalked my name on the board near the pool tables and took a place at the wall, alongside a shorter, muscular number wearing a pair of short overalls and no shirt.

"Don't you just hate the pretentiousness of some people," he said, without prompting. "I mean, you see that guy over there?" He pointed off in the direction of the dance floor, and I gave a polite glance that way, with my attention more focused on him, as cruising technique and etiquette demanded.

Ignoring the cruise for the moment, he continued, "He said his name was 'Amerigo.' *Amerigo*. Can you believe it? What kind of name is that?"

I instantly thought of Amerigo Vespucci, the Italian navigator and explorer after whom our country had been named. "My name is Paul," I said. *You can't get much plainer than that*, I thought. "What's yours?"

The young man extended his hand. "Tryon," he replied.

"Pardon?" I had expected 'John' or some such.

"Tryon," he said again. "Pleased to meet you." His handshake — of the limp, boneless variety — was the last straw.

"I'll be right back," I lied, and I ducked out the bar's back door and headed for home.

Saturday morning, I pulled out my oversized, pinstriped jacket and slacks that I hoped would pass for Mr. Spock's gangster attire from the classic Trek episode called "A Piece of the Action." I had heard that die-hard Trekkies — or "Trekkers," as they now preferred to be called — could be real sticklers for detail. You wouldn't be caught dead wearing a third-season *Next Generation* uniform with *first*-season rank collar pips, for example. Or you couldn't expect to get away with wearing a classic Trek outfit, carrying a second show weapon.

As I got dressed, though, I couldn't help recalling that episode of Saturday Night Live in which guest-host William Shatner played himself attending one of these conventions as many cast members often do, and when grilled a little too much by nit-picking fans, he snapped and shouted from his podium for them to get a life.

"Not bad," I said, admiring the look in the mirror that hung on the bathroom door. I held up my Vulcan ears for the full effect, then pocketed them until I got to Otto's house.

"Attack mode, Dante," I said to the dog, closing the door.

Fifteen minutes later, I pulled my Jeep behind Otto's borrowed *Times* van in his driveway and bounded up the steps to his front door.

"Permission to come aboard, Captain," I said when he answered in full Starfleet attire.

"Granted, Number One," Nicholson played back. "Step into my ready room."

In the short time I had known him, I had never been inside his house, and stepping into the foyer, I was immediately impressed. The front door emptied into a large, sunken living room, dominated by his legendary saltwater aquarium that took up the better part of the far wall.

"Wow," I mouthed as I walked over to it.

It had to be at least five hundred gallons, and he had painstakingly decorated it with live corals and sculpted rock edifices that gave it the look of an actual reef. In a clearing of sand about four feet across stood a number of algae-covered pillars, giving the undersea oasis the notion of the ruins of Atlantis.

A small leopard-spotted shark glided along the bottom. From behind a cluster of rocks, a snowflake moray eel poked out its head, mouth open, breathing rhythmically, showing its teeth. Half a dozen royal blue damselfish schooled in the tank's mid-waters, swimming tightly together.

"I've never seen captive saltwater fish school like that before," I said, knowing that the practice was rarely seen in the in-home aquarium.

"There's safety in numbers," Otto replied. He pointed to the black scorpionfish he had bought the last time we had been at PetCo. It swept through the water overhead, fins fanned out majestically, fearing nothing. Otto opened one of the doors in the tank stand's lower cabinet, revealing a dimly lit five-gallon tank, teeming with feeder goldfish. With a sweep of a small net, he fished out three and, opening the lid of the tank above, he dropped them in. "I have to keep Picard well-fed," he said as the scorpionfish rotated one of its independently moving eyes on its breakfast, and with a sweep of its tail then maneuvered its way over to gobble two instantly. "Or he may decide that the damsels would make a nice snack."

"Picard?" I asked. "Like the fish that Jean-Luc kept in his ready room on the Enterprise-D."

"Precisely. And that's Jabba," he said, pointing to the moray. "And this is Bullwinkle."

"Your octopus," I said. I leaned over to peer into the section of the tank Otto had glassed off to house his latest addition. If I didn't know any better, I'd say the creature's cave was just that: a cave made out of the natural arrangements of the rock. But a closer look showed that was an illusion, since he had surrounded the separate tank-within-the-tank with various anemone-covered rocks and plants. The wall that divided it from the rest of the self-contained waterworld was barely visible. Inside, a catlike eye looked back at me, amid a mass of suction-cupped tentacles. Its left blowvalve pulsed silently. Its eye widened, its skin flushed a darker brown, and its blue bands around its tentacles glowed when it felt I was getting too close.

"Beautiful," I breathed. I stepped back to take it all in. "What's that one's name?" I asked, pointing to a copperbanded butterfly fish.

"I haven't bothered to name any others," he said simply. "So, do you want the rest of the tour before we attach your ears and go?"

"Sure," I said, and the next few minutes were spent passing through his kitchen, an elaborate study, and exercise room, and two bedrooms. The decor was simple but comfortable, and it — along with Otto's relaxed manner — made me feel at home.

After adhering my Vulcan ears and donning the necessary hairpiece over my flattop, Otto handed me the Tommy gun he had promised, completing the outfit.

"You sure you want to keep the mustache?" he asked. "Spock never had one."

"No," I said, "but I do. The mustache stays."

"Suit yourself," he said. Picking up what I'm sure was a regulation, fourth-season phazer and attaching it to his belt, he gave us both one final look of approval, then gestured to the door. "Engage."

After a forty-five minute drive into San Francisco, we parked in an all-day lot in the Embarcadero and walked over to the Regency where the convention was taking place. Along the way, we intercepted three Klingons, a Romulan, and a gaggle of Cardasians.

"This is going to be fun," I said, and together the Captain and I took an escalator up to the Registration level.

We spent the better part of the morning attending lectures on Starfleet propulsion systems, upcoming season's episodes for the *Next Generation*, and the ongoing debate on who was the more formidable Federation captain — Kirk or Picard. One of the highlights came when we took our seats in a large auditorium for a chance to hear DeForest Kelley, a.k.a. Doctor "Bones" McCoy, reminisce on his "five year mission" on television and the film's version of the U.S.S. Enterprise.

Stepping to the podium wearing an old blue T-shirt, a sport coat, and jeans, Kelley took in a round of thunderous applause, then moved to speak into the microphone. When his first few words broke into a wave of static, he yanked the thing from its stand, and yelled clearly to the sound man backstage, "Take care of this. I'm a doctor, dammit, not an audio technician!"

The laughter and sparse clapping that followed continued as the embarrassed sound tech crept on stage to replace the mic.

"It's dead, Jim," DeForest Kelley said in classic "Bones" McCoy fashion, as he handed it over. Moments later, with all having been set right in this universe, he treated us to half an hour of Trek tales and anecdotes, then endured about ten minutes of fan's questions.

Afterwards, when Otto and I had stepped over to a water fountain outside the main hall, I had a rather tall man with a beard ask me, "Do you know where the Farallon Room is?"

I answered as best I could, and he was off. As Otto came up from his drink, he looked at me and said, "I'm impressed. You didn't wig out in usual Trekkie style when Jonathan Frakes spoke to you. You're smooth."

"*The* Jonathan Frakes?" I asked. "Lieutenant Riker on the *Next Generation*? It didn't look anything like him."

"That was him all right," Otto confirmed. "He does look a lot taller in person, though. And I think he's put on some weight."

"That *was* him, wasn't it? Jonathan Frakes."

"Come on," Otto said. "Let's hit one of the collector's rooms before all the good stuff is gone."

Inside one of the larger convention rooms stood a number of tables containing anything that could ever pass as Star Trek memorabilia.

There were Tribbles, comic books, and uniforms. Limited edition collector's plates with images of nearly every cast member or ship, some autographed, for a higher price. Posters adorned the walls behind the stands, and some tradespeople sold copies of the show's teleplays or their own original works, unauthorized by the Star Trek powers that be. I think they called them "The Borg."

Some merchants wore costumes, and they tended to have more customers. Others carried collectibles from other sci-fi films such as *Star Wars* or television epics like "Lost In Space." I even saw a "Land of the Giants" lunch box like the one I had as a kid. The guy wanted $125.00 for it.

I looked over to find Otto engaged in an in-depth conversation with a merchant in Ferengi attire. He was showing the creature the phazer he had brought with him, and in standard Ferengi manner, the guy was trying to buy it from him.

"This isn't like any of the others I've seen," the Ferengi said. "So detailed, so realistic." Weighing it in his hand, he said, "It even feels like the real thing. How much?"

"It's not for sale," Otto said. "I made it myself, using Starfleet-issue schematics."

When I turned to the table in front of me, I spied a "Starfleet Academy" bumper sticker that I simply had to have.

"What are you charging for this?" I asked the woman behind the register.

"Two Federation credits," she said. "That's two earth dollars to you, my dear Vulcan."

I blushed, having forgotten my get-up. "Thank you," I said, handing her a pair of ones. As I did so, I looked about half a foot over and stared into the face of serial killer Jeffrey Dahmer. "Is that what I think it is?" I asked. I picked up the small packet, a bundle of bubble-gum-sized cards, with the drawing of one of the most infamous people of all crime on top.

"Serial Killer Trading Cards," she said. "Yep. That's them. You know, they were never issued as a set, but my husband and I tore through a zillion of the individual packets until we got them all."

The cards were wrapped tightly in plastic, so all I could see was Dahmer's image, set against a yellow-and-gray background, with red blood splattered across it. "JEFFREY DAHMER" it read along the bottom in bold, black print. The artwork was better than I had expected, in fact, it easily rivaled some of the stuff they were putting on postage stamps these days. I turned the packet over to read the back of the last card, Number 110, which was a checklist of all of those contained in the deck.

"I'll take these too," I said, almost afraid to ask how much they were.

"That'd be twenty-seven credits," she said. She slid the items in a small brown bag for me. "Total."

I gave her thirty more and told her to keep it.

"Spending your hard earned cash, my friend?"

I turned around to face Otto and blushed again. "Just a little something for the car," I said, flashing the end of the bumper sticker as it stuck out of the bag. "How about you?"

"Nah," he said. "I'm about through here. How about you?"

"Ready when you are, Captain."

"Make it so," he said.

On our way out the merchant's room door, Otto stopped at a table near the standing Captain Kirk Cardboard cut-out. He flipped through a handful of Xeroxed copies of various movie and TV scripts, then landed on a thin, 25-page manuscript.

"I can't believe it," he said. "I've finally found one."

"What is it?" I asked. Over his shoulder I read the typewritten cover sheet: "TEARS OF THE SUN by Stephen James White."

"It's the original short-story that inspired the current best-seller of the same name," he said. "Mr. White had written the piece in high school for the National Council for the Teachers of Written English back in 1979. With it, he made it to the finals and received some certificate or other nonsense. Fourteen years later, he dusted it off, regressed about 30 years before the time in which this story takes place, and created the now-known novel on the shelves today. It'd be interesting to see what germinated such a phenomenal best-seller. Imagine finding fame today with something you had once created as a boy."

"Some guys have all the luck," I said.

Otto paid the man at the table ten dollars, and with that, we were on our way home.

When I pulled into his drive, I reached for the brown paper bag I had gotten at the Con. "You know," I said, "I wanted to thank you for all the guidance you've given me since I came on staff, so I bought you a little something."

"The bumper sticker?" he asked.

"No," I said, a little embarrassed. "That's mine. Inside."

Otto pulled the wrapped deck of serial killer trading cards out, and he lit up ear to ear. "You found these, too," he exclaimed. "Why today has been just a glorious day, hasn't it? Thank you, Paul." He opened the package and fanned through the cards. "These are more amazing than I had hoped. Look. Charles Manson," he said, holding up Manson's image. "And here's Kenneth Bianchi's. The one who's suing the makers. He doesn't even have a whole card. He's sharing it with his accomplice, Angelo Buono. I don't see why he's so upset." He laughed. "And here's John Wayne Gacy, complete with clown make-up. And David Berkowitz, the 'Son of Sam.' Paul, this is truly a thoughtful gift. Thank you again."

"You're welcome," I said, smiling back. I handed him the Tommy Gun he'd let me borrow and said, "Here. And thanks."

"You can keep the hair piece," he said, getting out. "It's you."

"Great," I laughed. "See you on Monday." I put the Jeep in reverse.

Holding up his hand in a Vulcan "V" salute, he left me with, "Live long, Paul, and prosper."

After getting home to change clothes and walk the dog, I drove over to the *Times* office to spend the rest of the afternoon digging up whatever I could find on the late Nicholas Pirelli.

I started by reviewing all that had been written in yesterday's afternoon edition and was relieved to find that no mention of the way the body was discovered had been made.

I still had a chance.

With any luck, I'd crack this story wide open and have my by-line on something bigger than the *Times*'s legendary Garrison Fitzgerald ever dreamed about. Wheeling a chair up to the old microfilm viewer in the newspaper morgue, I opened a nearby drawer and searched for the reel that would contain the past articles on the Pirelli scandal. I found it, slightly out of order with the other reels, and carefully threaded the machine.

***

Hunter Whitloe spent his Saturday questioning the neighbors on the block where Antonio Tyger and his family lived, after a thorough search of their home had given him little to go on. By the time the ambulance for Deputy Samuels had arrived yesterday, Antonio and any one else who resided there managed to clear out. A few opened drawers and disheveled closets revealed they had packed a few things before they left, and one of the closets in the master bedroom had been gutted out entirely.

Through his conversation with the elderly man next door, Whitloe found out that Antonio lived with his parents and an older brother who was some kind of drop-out. For the most part, the Tygers kept to themselves, but, the neighbor said, they did tend to have a great number of quiet, late night visitors.

"Antonio was never one to be in any sort of trouble though," the man had told Whitloe. "I always thought he'd be the one to make it through school, and make something of himself. That job he had delivering newspapers was teaching him some responsibility. That's more than I can say for his good-for-nothing older brother or his dad."

"Thank you for your time," the detective said, making a few notes on a pad.

After his door-to-door survey of the houses on that block, Whitloe called the *Times* to confirm what an early-morning stake-out of his had already told him: the kid hadn't gone on his route this morning, and they had to scramble to find a replacement to get the papers delivered at a reasonable time. Most of them had arrived late anyway, resulting in a litany of calls to the Complaint Desk.

A trip to Antonio's father's place of employment — one of the refineries in Martinez — turned out to be a bust, too. He had been laid off two weeks ago, and they hadn't seen him since he had picked up his final paycheck.

No one could recall if Mrs. Tyger held down a job, but most doubted it since she had had her left arm amputated after an automobile accident, and she spent most of her time doped up on painkillers.

Everyone knew that Antonio's older brother, Charles, couldn't keep a steady job, and most wouldn't be found within one hundred yards of any place of leisure he might frequent, even if they knew of any, which they didn't.

That evening, Whitloe made a trip to Mercy Hospital to visit his wounded deputy, but Samuels's condition was still grave enough that he remained under sedation and couldn't be questioned. When he returned Sunday morning, however, he camped out at the foot of the man's bed, determined to make some progress in something.

"How ya feeling?" Whitloe asked when Samuels finally opened his eyes.

"Like shit," he said. "Like I've been shot."

Whitloe forced a laugh. "Did you see who did this?" he asked.

Samuels shook his head weakly.

"Well, we're on top of it, so don't you worry about it. Just get some rest."

"Lieutenant," the deputy whispered as Whitloe rose to leave, "sorry to leave you in the lurch like this. I know you could use me right about now."

Whitloe raised a hand. "Don't worry, man. I'm following up on your Tyger lead, and I've got Briggs and Burton doing their part, too. And, hey, you'll be up and around in no time, I'm sure."

Samuels gave a thumbs up and strained a smile.

Whitloe's smile was strained, too, but not because he'd been shot.

"I was beginning to worry that you wouldn't be home in time," Gladys Whitloe said as her husband returned around five. "You'd better get dressed."

"'Dressed'?" he repeated. "Dressed for what?"

"Our Bridge game with Geneva and Clyde Todd, silly. It's at seven."

Hunter groaned in displeasure. "Ah, hon, I'm exhausted. Do we have to?"

"Hunter," she said sternly, "you've backed out of the last two games. I won't let you do it again."

Whitloe opened the refrigerator and took out a pint of ice cream. "But I don't like Geneva, Gladys. You know that. That old bat gets on my last good nerve, and after the week I've had, I'm not sure that one isn't shot, too."

Gladys followed her husband into the kitchen. "I don't care, Hunter. Geneva's my best friend, and I enjoy spending time with her. I'm one of the few friends she has from the old clan, when she was married to Spencer, until he died. . ."

"Two years ago," he said, finishing her sentence. "Yadda, yadda, yadda. I know the story." He dug a spoon into the ice cream and took a bite. He continued to speak with his mouth full. "You know, I thought old Spencer's death would have mellowed the bitch in her out a little, but if it did, I don't see it. She's still as nosy and as crotchety as ever. And I think she only married this Todd fellow because he had money and no spine to speak of. Have you listened to the way she talks to him? It's like he. . ."

"Hunter Stewart Whitloe," Gladys said, using his full name as she did whenever she got angry, which wasn't often at all. "I will not have you speak that way about that woman, and yes, you are going with me to play cards tonight. I don't care how tired you are."

"Yes, dear," he said.

"Now go in there and put on some decent clothes."

"Yes, dear," he said again, but he did not move.

"And put that ice cream away this instant. You'll spoil the dinner that Geneva's making for us."

Whitloe moaned. "She's cooking again?" he asked, although *cooking* wasn't a word usually applied to what Geneva Todd did with food in the kitchen. "Can't we pick up something on the way?"

"We'll do no such thing," Gladys said, taking the pint container from her husband's hand and returning it to the freezer. "Now, get a move on."

"Yes, dear."

At the Todd residence, Hunter suffered through a meal of blackened meatloaf by trying to drown out the charred taste with ketchup. His wife helped Geneva clear the table afterward for the card game, and he and Clyde Todd waited out in the living room with a couple of beers.

"So, it's off to Arizona again tomorrow, eh, Clyde?" Whitloe said, making small talk about the man's job that had him travel often. He never really cared to know what the man did, so he never asked.

"That's right," Clyde said. He set his beer on a nearby end table and picked up his pipe, stuffing it with a cherry tobacco, then lighting it. "Arizona."

"I can't believe it's been almost a year," Gladys said to Geneva as they came in from the kitchen. "You and Clyde, I mean. Tell me, is it any different the second time around? I mean, you were with Spencer what, fifty years?"

Geneva walked Gladys over to her second marriage certificate that she had recently framed. "Well, you know, Spencer and I married rather young, and we really didn't know anything. And times were different back then, too. 'Til death do you part' meant just that. None of this divorce nonsense, not like today. We had some rough times, but we always managed to make it through them. 'Through sickness and in health', too. Like the year before he died when I developed that heart condition. Remember how he rallied the townsfolk together to come up with the money for my pacemaker surgery? That man was a saint. He taught me a lot."

"That was an amazing time," Gladys recalled, having written a check for five hundred dollars for the cause herself. "But your standing as the county librarian had made you known throughout the town as well. I'm sure that helped a little."

"Oh, no," she said modestly. "It was all Spencer's doing, and I'm here today as testament to it. And let me tell you, I wouldn't come out of retirement to work in that old library again for all the tea in China."

With both hands, she straightened the framed certificate for her marriage to her second husband. Gladys smiled as she read it: On this 23rd day of August, 1992, Mr. Clyde Arthur Todd and Mrs. Geneva Francesca Graham entered into holy matrimony. . .

"I married my dear Clyde knowing a lot more now than I did back then," Geneva Todd said. She moved over to him and took him by the arm. "So, I guess, in answer to your original question, Gladys, yes, it *is* different the second time around. For instance, Clyde comes from a family with ten brothers and sisters, and that certainly took some getting used to. Spencer was an only child."

"Ten? Oh, my," Gladys said. "That's a houseful."

Through the smoke of his pipe, Clyde smiled broadly. "We're all very close, too. You don't see that a lot in families these days."

"Isn't that the truth?" Gladys added. "You know, Hunter and his older brother, Clayton, haven't spoken in over six years."

"You've got to be kidding," Geneva said. "Hunter, why?"

"If you don't mind," Whitloe said, "I'd rather not discuss it."

That answer didn't seem to satisfy Clyde Todd. He chimed in with, "Come on, man. What would have you not be close to a member of your own family. . . your brother, for gosh sakes?"

If Hunter Whitloe hated one thing more than someone who wouldn't mind their own business it was someone who wouldn't swear. Clyde Todd seemed to be both at the moment. He said nothing until Geneva chirped, "Whatever it is, or was, Hunter, you should just let it go. Here," she said, handing him their telephone receiver. "Call him right now, if you'd like."

Hunter took the phone from her and slammed it back into the cradle. "I said I don't care to have this conversation. Not now. Not here. And certainly not with you."

"Hunter!" Gladys said.

He turned to her and stuck an index finger in her face. "Don't push this, Gladys. My brother's lies and what he's done has disgraced my entire family, and I don't know that I can ever forgive him for it. I looked up to him once, but now I don't even know who he is anymore."

"He's your *brother*," she tried. "He's still the same Clayton Whitloe."

"And who is that?" Hunter replied. "Look," he said, pulling back. "I'm not about to go into this with these complete strangers. Now get your coat. We're leaving."

"But the Bridge match," Clyde said.

"I'm in no mood for card games, Clyde. I think your wife's attempt at meatloaf has given me the raging shits. Now, if you'll excuse us, we'd like to be on our way."

Gladys retreated to the bedroom and retrieved their jackets, and when she returned, she meekly handed Hunter his. "I'm so sorry," she tried to say to Geneva.

"Don't apologize for me," Hunter snapped. "I'll be out in the car."

The ride home was a silent one, and when they finally crawled into bed together, Hunter didn't bother to kiss his wife goodnight. After about half an hour, he was able to drift off to sleep, but this night, he tossed and turned more than ever before.

Chapter Seven

Back at the Honeycomb Hideout

"YOU'RE IN AWFULLY EARLY for a Monday."

Turning from the microfilm viewer, I saw Otto Nicholson standing there in the newspaper morgue's doorway. The machine spat out another sheet of background information on Nicholas Pirelli. I added it to the stack of pages I'd been collecting over the weekend. I'd left only to grab something to eat or to go home and sleep, and this morning I was back before the sun had come up. "No rest for the wicked," I replied.

"Did Charlotte give you another assignment?" he asked. "Good for you. I knew she'd get over it sooner or later. Anyway, I came in to tell you that you've got a phone call. Line two."

"Thanks," I said. Scooping together my research, I got up and made it back to my desk. "Paul Blazer here," I said, picking up the receiver.

"Where the heck have you been? It's been three days!" came the voice.

"Pamela," I said. "I'm sorry. Things got rather hectic here, and. . ."

"Well, I've done a little nosing around here when I couldn't get a hold of you, and you'll never believe what I found out."

"What?" I readied a pen and searched for a piece of paper.

"Remember all the security that accompanied Artie Kellogg?" she asked, with a pause for effect. "From what Mr. Brandriff says, they were here because the kid had received some sort of death threat."

Kellogg, I wrote. "Uh-huh."

"Did you hear what I said? Someone threatened to kill the guy."

"Any idea who it might have been?" I asked, keeping my cool.

"No," she said. "But after his little show on Friday morning, the police left as mysteriously as they came. Now, if someone had promised to murder Artie Kellogg, wouldn't you think he'd get more than a couple of days of police protection? Hell, if somebody had threatened *my life*, I'd put up quite a stink if my bodyguard just up and left like that."

Not if you both knew that the threat was over, I thought. *Like somebody else was killed instead.*

"Have you been able to talk with Kellogg?" I asked.

"No. He was only scheduled to be in town a few days," she said. "He checked out of his hotel room Friday afternoon."

Damn, I thought. *No telling what the kid would have been able to tell me. . .*

"But he does have a girlfriend in town," Pamela continued. "And I took the liberty of calling her on Saturday. He's there, all right. But he's supposed to leave some time today. I asked him to wait until he was able to speak with you."

"Pamela, you're an angel," I said. I took down the girl's name, address, and phone number, then said, "Thanks. I'll get over there right away."

"You owe me for this, Blazer," she said.

"Anything," I replied. "Well, anything but a pepper spray class."

Pamela laughed. "Too late. I did that one on Sunday. But I'll come up with something."

"I'm sure you will. Gotta run. I'll let you know how this turns out, okay?"

"Sure. Just be careful."

"No problem," I said, signing off. "Thanks again. Bye."

"You're becoming quite the workaholic," Otto Nicholson said as I hung up the phone. "It reminds me a little of Garry."

"Fitzgerald?" I asked.

"Yeah. He'd always come in to supervise the morning press run, and he'd never leave until well after midnight." Otto gave a chuckle, remembering. "We used to grab a quick bite for breakfast and eat it right here at my desk."

"That reminds me," I said. "I forgot to eat this morning. I'm going to run and get something." Standing, I folded Artie Kellogg's girlfriend's address and tucked it into my pocket. "Need anything?"

"I'm fine," he said.

"If anyone misses me, I should be back in a couple of hours."

Within ten minutes, Kellogg's girlfriend, Jennifer, had let me into her parent's living room, and she was calling for him.

"He was in the shower," she said. "It was nice of you to call before coming over."

I had hit a pay phone on the way, having heard one of my mother's lectures on manners in my head when I put the key in the ignition of my Jeep. "No problem. I'm just glad he's still here to talk to."

"Hey, there," came a voice behind me. Artie Kellogg met me wearing an old pair of jeans, no shirt, and running a towel through his wet hair.

I gave his free hand a firm shake. "I'm Paul Blazer, of the Chestnut Grove *Times*," I began, without giving my official position or title. "Flunkie" or "Gopher" wouldn't have commanded much respect, I suppose.

"Pleased to meet you," Kellogg said. "Have a seat."

***

Lieutenant Detective Hunter Whitloe's morning started with an ass-chewing from Captain Colm Atherton, behind the closed doors of his office.

"We've got three people dead, Hunter, and I need some answers," the Captain said. "What have we got so far?"

"I plan to follow up with Taggert and Malone this afternoon," Whitloe replied. "Hopefully, the Pirelli autopsy will give us a few new leads."

"*Hope* isn't going to solve this thing, Detective, and right now, our luck's going down the shitter. What's happening down at the lab?"

"All the cereal's come back clean," he said. "No trace of any poison. We're still running that one latent print through AFIS, which may take another week or so." Whitloe flipped through a page or two of his file on the councilman's murder. "The items found at the last crime scene gave us little more than a few nice pieces of kitchenware and one slightly frazzled hooker. The tests on Pirelli probably will show an elevated level of nicotine in his system, just like Black and Totah, but that shouldn't come as any big surprise. You ever see the man on TV after that scandal broke out?"

Atherton nodded his head. "He hardly said Word One between those drags on his cancer sticks."

"Lung cancer would've killed him if this joker hadn't come along sooner," Whitloe noted. "Still no sign of that Tyger kid. I've got watches set up on his morning paper route and at his school if he shows up."

"What about Briggs?" the Captain asked.

The detective bent his head to look over a few pages of notes as he said, "I've got him checking on a possible link with the cereal manufacturer. All the boxes have been General Mills products, and that could mean something." He kept his head down for half a minute longer than was necessary, wondering if the Captain would see a small red streak in his chin if he looked up again.

"Good," he said. "How's Samuels doing?"

"Better. I stopped by Mercy this morning on my way in."

"What about the last clue we got on Friday?"

"Golden Grahams," Whitloe said. "I'm running a check on all the Grahams listed in the Chestnut Grove phone directory and cross-referencing them with people with that last name who get the morning edition of the *Times*."

"Good thinking. Let me know if any of them show up on this kid Tyger's route."

"I plan to."

"You'd better do more than plan, Hunter. You'd better make some serious progress — and I'm talking an *arrest* — pretty damn soon. We've started to get some heat from a few of my superiors, and you know how much I like that. We've been pretty lucky keeping most of this from the press so far, but I'm not sure how much longer that luck will last."

"Yes, sir," Whitloe said. He got up to leave.

"Hunter," Atherton said softly, "I don't need to remind you that shit rolls down hill. If this thing blows up and hits the papers or TV, we could end up looking like fools. A *cereal* killer. Jesus!" He turned away slightly for his next line, one that Hunter took more as a promise than a threat. "And if someone has to go down for this, I want you to know that it won't be me."

Whitloe said nothing but nodded once, understanding. As he left the Captain's office, he decided to make his trip to the coroner's earlier than originally planned. It was about time to put fire under a few people before the one under him charred his ass.

***

"I'm running to the mail room," Otto said, passing my desk. "Got anything?"

I looked up from my notes from my interview with Artie Kellogg, now half an hour old. "Nope. Maybe later though." I watched as he wheeled a metal cart around the office, filling it along the way.

The information Kellogg had given me had raised more questions than answers. He said he'd been placed in protective custody the moment he reached town last Wednesday, and a police detective shared the adjoining room at his hotel, shadowing him whenever he left. The detective had been somewhat vague, but explained that they were concerned for his safety, given the high publicity his upcoming assembly had received in the press. He also said they had reason to suspect that his life had actually been threatened.

That's where things got even sketchier.

Kellogg said that they never really told him what the threat had been or who they suspected had made it, just some mention that it had to do with his notoriety and the fact he dealt with kids. When he tried to lighten the mood by ordering a bowl of Trix cereal from room service, the detective had freaked and tackled the young man sent up from the kitchen.

"I thought, 'Silly rabbit. . .Trix are for kids,'" he had said to me. "And I work with kids, so when I saw it on the menu, I couldn't resist. Jeez, he was so uptight."

But Trix had been present at the Pirelli crime scene, I thought. Lucky Lucy had told me so. If somehow the Trix had been a clue. . .

Wait a minute.

I tore through my notes on the Matthew Black death. My article had said he'd choked to death.

On *Wheaties*.

Back issues I had dug up told me he'd once endorsed the stuff, but he lost the contract with General Mills when it was discovered he didn't like the product. I had tried to put that information in my sidebar on him, but it had been nixed by Assistant News Editor Charlotte Journigan.

Why?

What if this cereal thing was more than some strange coincidence?

Both Matthew Black and Nicholas Pirelli were found dead with it. Both had once been on Chestnut Grove's short list of popular and famous residents.

I sat for a moment and tried to piece it all together.

Black. Olympic wannabe. Wheaties.

Pirelli. Prostitutes. Trix.

There certainly seemed to be *that* connection. That all made sense. But if it were that simple, why hadn't it been Kellogg rather than Pirelli?

Kellogg. Kids. Trix.

That seemed to follow just as well as the former councilman's pattern. Something else was missing.

Scandal, I thought. Both Black and Pirelli had been involved in some sort of prior scandal that had ruined their careers.

But Artie Kellogg had just as powerfully ruined *his* future with his DUI, hadn't he? Maybe that wasn't it. I sorted through the last week's worth of *Times* early morning editions to see if there was something else I had missed. I passed backwards over the Pirelli piece that ran on Friday. . . Kellogg's article came out on Thursday. . .another Kellogg preview on Wednesday, then. . .

My eyes froze on the small column of space devoted to the passing of former fitness guru Terry Totah. That had been the piece

Charlotte had taken from me and given to the college co-op to write on Tuesday. Out of anger, I hadn't read it.

Until now.

It was simple, more of an ode to a friend than a news article, with no note of how the man had died. But if I remember correctly, he had been found by the fitness show's producer, in the morning,

In the morning, I thought, *like all the others.*

I made a note. I needed to talk with this guy. Now, what was his name?

Shawn. . .No, Shannon. . .I was drawing a blank. Shannon *what*?!

And I had given all of my notes on Totah to the college co-op Laney.

Think, Blazer. Think.

Shannon Whats-his-name had called because he and the crew of the. . .

"Public Access Cable station," I muttered to myself, writing it down. They had called to pay for the man's obit, since he had no real family to speak of. The cable station, I thought again. I could reach him through that.

Getting up, I walked over to the file cabinet where we kept the local phone books. I didn't want to risk getting caught using telephone information because those calls eventually showed up as toll charges on the company bill. With my luck, someone would decide to look a little too closely next month, and. . .

Here it was. I copied the number down on a sheet of paper.

Through the nearby door, I could hear Charlotte's voice as she spoke sternly into her phone.

"Quit stonewalling me, Malone. I thought we were friends. Just tell me what your office found when you opened up that scumbag Pirelli. I know you don't have any definite answers yet, but. . .ah, don't give me that. . .come on, Malone. . .I don't care what. . ." Then I heard her slam down the receiver and say, "Shit." What followed sounded like papers ruffling, then her door swung open and she yelled, "Blazer!" until she saw that I was standing only two feet away.

I quickly folded the sheet with my number on it and put away the phone book. "Yes, ma'am."

"Oh, there you are," she said, her voice far less deafening. "Nicholson skipped me when he went around for mail. Could you run these down for me?" She handed me a short stack of padded envelopes, letters, and brown-wrapped packages.

"Sure," I said, pocketing my phone number and freeing both hands to take her lot. "No problem."

"You're a dear," she said in the tone she used whenever she got her way. "Be sure they send them First Class. All of it. I have deadlines to meet, too, you know."

***

Hunter Whitloe and coroner Tess Taggert stood over the remains of former councilman Nicholas Pirelli, which had been cut, sliced, and examined every which way but inside out.

"Nothing in the stomach," Whitloe said, repeating what Toe Tag had just confirmed. "So this joker's force-feeding the cereal after his victim's dead."

"Or while he's dying," Taggert said. "Or maybe he kills them just after he's ordered them to start eating."

"So he comes in with some weapon," the detective said, following through. "A gun, or something."

"Perhaps."

"But none of these guys have been shot."

"No. There's no real physical trauma to the body of any kind. You know we haven't been able to isolate any poison, and I'll be damned if I can find a needle mark anywhere."

Setting down her case file, she stretched on a pair of rubber gloves.

"So, some sort of lethal injection is out, too," Whitloe said.

"I can't find any evidence for it," she said. "And another thing that's got me stumped is this." She rolled Pirelli's head to the side to reveal a small, red welt just inside the hairline on the back of his neck.

"What's that?" Whitloe asked. "A hickey?"

"Not unless that prostitute who found him is into something really kinky."

With gloved hands, the detective brushed at the hair to get a better look. "She told me she didn't touch him, before or after she found him."

"So that rules out getting this through some amorous event," Taggert said. "It would be funny though. The kiss of death." She laughed.

"What could it be?"

The coroner consulted her notes. "I found something similar on Matthew Black. Remember? We dismissed it as a reaction to the patch."

"Did Totah have one, too?" Whitloe asked, hoping.

"No."

"That's a rather odd place to put the patch, wouldn't you say?"

"If it hadn't been in the hairline, I'd have to say no," she replied. "You can't put it in the same place when you change to a new one. Prolonged contact, especially on the same place time after time, would cause a rash."

Whitloe pointed to the back of the corpse's head. "Like this."

"But you want direct and total contact with the skin, Hunter. You wouldn't put it over hair."

"Okay, okay. Let's rule out the patch for the moment. What else could it be?"

The morgue's door opened, and in strode Redford Malone. "You're not going to like this, Lieutenant," he said.

"What now?"

"I just got off the phone with Charlotte Journigan, assistant news editor at the *Times*. She's hungry for something."

Whitloe's lungs angrily pushed out some air. "You didn't *feed* her anything, I hope."

"No, sir," Malone said. "But I'm not sure how much longer we can keep this quiet."

"Just do your damnedest," the detective said. "Or so help me God, you'll be next." With that, he marched past the other man and headed over to the Criminalistics Lab in Martinez.

Deputy Jonathan Briggs crossed another name off his list of local stores that carried any General Mills products.

"Seven down," he said to Birdie Burton, who stood beside him.

"Only about a hundred and seven to go," she finished.

"You know, this might go a little faster if we had some idea of what or who we were looking for."

Burton looked at him. "Jon, did you ever get the feeling that Lieutenant Whitloe gave you this assignment just to keep us busy?"

Briggs furrowed his brow and pondered the thought for a moment. "No. Why would he do that?"

***

"I'm sorry, Mister, uh. . .Blazer, was it?"

"Yes," I replied. "Paul Blazer. Of the *Times*." I brought the telephone mouthpiece closer, in case the woman at the local cable access station just couldn't hear me.

"I got that part," she said. "And again, I'm sorry. Mr. McMillan isn't in. He took a couple of days off after Mr. Totah's funeral. I don't expect him back until Wednesday or Thursday. But I have your number. I'll have him return your call as soon as he's in."

"Thank you," I said. "Have him try me at home if it's after business hours."

"Will do," she said. "Good bye."

Otto Nicholson came by my desk just as I hung up. "Come on, my friend. It's time for our lunch time run."

Stalled for the moment, I said, "Sure. I could use the exercise. Maybe it'll help clear my head." I stood and followed him to the Men's Room to change.

***

At the Criminalistics Lab, technician Sydney Pincus gave Hunter some news.

"We've got a positive match on that latent fingerprint you lifted from Matthew Black's neck," he said, and he watched the detective light up for a moment. "It's exactly like the one you'd find on his own left hand. Index finger, to be precise. He must have reached to his throat as he was choking." He made the motion himself, bringing both hands to his own neck. "It's rather instinctual, actually."

"Great," Whitloe said. "What about the print from the cereal box?"

"Nothing on that one yet," Pincus said. "But we have been able to rule out you detective, and everyone else in your station. We have all of those prints on file, as a matter of practice. It's a shame we don't have such a file for all those sociopaths out there. That would make my job much easier."

Whitloe felt like reenacting Pincus's choking demonstration once again, but with a little more force than he had used on himself a moment before. "Any preliminary results from the Pirelli tissue samples?" he asked instead.

Pincus consulted his files. "Nicotine," he said. "As you expected. But the guy was a chain smoker, you know."

"Yeah. I know."

The day was half over, and the detective had a sinking feeling that he wasn't going to get anything else done in the time remaining. When he left the lab, he checked in at the station to get the progress on his Graham phone book/newspaper route cross.

Nothing.

Not a single match.

To be on the safe side, he ordered half a dozen officers to each of the six Grahams that had been listed in the directory. They were to quietly sit in an unmarked patrol car from now until tomorrow, noon, and to report anything that might be construed as suspicious.

He just hoped that there wasn't a Mr. Graham out there with an unlisted number.

While talking with dispatch, he received word that Briggs hadn't come up with anything either. Not that he expected much with that one.

"Tell him to keep looking," he said. "It's probably the strongest lead we've got going right now." He winced a little as he said that, realizing that it was very true at the moment.

***

I had spent the rest of my afternoon researching the handful of elderly people who had passed away at the local nursing home facility. Chestnut Grove's Twilight Home, dubbed "Twilight Zone" by everyone at the paper, reported their deaths on a weekly basis, and by now, they would fax the listing directly to me. Today's was three pages, and it kept me busy, with little time to consider my notes on Black, Totah, and Pirelli.

When I made it home, I pulled a letter from my mailbox and shuddered a little when I saw that it had come from my ex, Scott, in Los Angeles. He wrote that he had spent the better part of the month in the hospital, having been stricken with toxoplasmosis. His T-cell count had fallen just below the 200-level, earning him an official diagnosis of AIDS. The doctors didn't expect him to last much longer than a year or two.

God, I thought. He had just learned he was HIV-positive last Christmas.

Three months ago.

How could a disease destroy someone so fast?

I immediately remembered that my own test results were now a little over a week away.

I tried to mentally prepare myself for the outcome, whatever it may be, but I found that there wasn't really that much that mattered to me at this moment.

Not even the possibility of solving what appeared to be a series of murders going on in my town. Nor the article that I would write afterwards.

"Want to go for a walk, Dante?" I asked the dog, too caught up in my own thoughts to try to talk to him in German.

We took a slow pace and circled around my neighborhood in about half an hour, then retreated inside for a quiet evening alone and an early start on sleep.

***

Whitloe got up Tuesday morning some time after five and stared at his tired face in the bathroom mirror. Trying to make the bags under his eyes less evident, he extended his jaw, stretching the muscles above his cheeks. When that didn't have a lasting effect, he splashed some cold water from the basin.

"Still not sleeping well, dear?" asked his wife as she stepped onto the tiled floor.

Whitloe grunted a reply, then reached for some eye drops in the cabinet. Leaning his head back, he squirted his left eye, then the right. He blinked, and a mixture of tears and the solution ran down his face.

"I know we haven't talked about it since Sunday," Gladys began, "but I wanted to say that I'm sorry about what happened."

Whitloe tried to brush his teeth, and as his wife spoke, he found that gritting became much easier.

"Geneva Graham called yesterday," she continued. "She wanted to be sure you knew how bad she felt, too, and. . ."

The detective stopped brushing in mid-stroke. "What did you say?" he garbled through a mouthful of toothpaste.

"I said, Geneva's very sorry. She feels simply awful that. . ."

"No, no, no. You said, 'Graham.'" he repeated "'Geneva *Graham*.'"

"Oh," Gladys said, with a little embarrassment in her tone. "Graham was her former name. You know, when she was married to old Spencer."

"For *fifty years*," Whitloe said, remembering the last piece. "*Golden*."

"Why, yes, but. . ."

Whitloe threw down his toothbrush and hocked a wad of paste into the sink. Grabbing a towel as he ran out of the bathroom, he wiped his mouth then pulled on yesterday's pair of pants and shirt, still hanging over the back of a chair. Next came his shoulder-holstered gun.

"Call the station, and have them send every available man over to Geneva Graham's place," he yelled. He fumbled with a pair of socks, but when they gave him too much trouble, he tossed them aside and slid his bare feet into his shoes.

"Hunter, what's. . .?" Gladys tried.

"Just do it!" he said, looking at his watch.

5:11.

He still had time.

"I'll try to get someone with the radio in the car, too," he said. "Well, don't just stand there!"

Gladys ran her slippered feet over to the phone and dialed as her husband ran out the front door.

5:27, Whitloe's watch read as he made it there in record time. Jumping from the car, he bounded up to the Todd's front door, and his eyes zeroed in on the small item on the welcome mat.

A copy of the *Times*.

He kicked the thing out of the way, then yanked on the screen door hard enough that the glass installed for the winter months shattered upon impact when it hit. He tried the main door's knob.

Locked.

As the screen door came back on its hinges and hit him in the shoulder, Whitloe thought he heard another door slam around the other side of the house.

"I got here as fast as I could, Lieutenant. What's. . ."

It was Briggs.

"Get over here, and help me with this," Hunter Whitloe bellowed. Together they lunged their full weight into the door. Once. . .twice. . .

On the third try, they forced the door open, wood splintering at the frame and the knob burying itself in the plaster of the inside wall.

"Over there," Briggs said, pointing toward a pair of feet visible from the doorway. Before he could make some sense of the scene, Whitloe had bolted past him and was kneeling in the kitchen, next to the body. The deputy felt his legs go weak. "Is she. . .?"

"Call 911," Hunter said. "She's still with us, but just barely." He gazed down at the fallen woman, cradling her head in his arm. "Hang on, Geneva. You're going to be just fine."

Geneva Graham-Todd took a great amount of strength to open her eyes and focus. As she did, she could see Hunter Whitloe looking past her, out of the room. "Hunter. . ." she said weakly.

The detective's gaze had fallen on the open box of cereal on the small dinette table, sitting next to a glass of orange juice and a bowl filled with Golden Grahams. "Geneva," he blurted, turning back her way, "Do you eat that stuff? The cereal? Is it yours?"

"Where's the ambulance?" Briggs yelled into the cordless phone he had found in the living room. "Well, have them move it!"

Geneva Graham coughed and winced, giving her head a small jerk to the side.

Hunter tried to read it. *Was that a nod or a shake*?

"Geneva," he repeated, "the *cereal*."

"It's my. . ." she tried. "My pa—"

"Her 'pay'?" Briggs repeated, dumbfounded.

"What was that Geneva?" Whitloe asked again.

"My pa—," she breathed out before her voice trailed off again.

"Her *pa*cemaker," the detective said, remembering her mechanically corrected heart condition. "Her *pacemaker*. Fuck!"

In that instant, he flashed on what he actually *should* be doing at that moment if this woman had not, in fact, been the serial killer's next intended victim, as he had thought.

"Stand back," he ordered Briggs. He lay the woman on the linoleum and readied himself for CPR. "Stand back, damn it!" he cursed, angrier at his own slow reaction than to his deputy's proximity.

Whitloe began the timed thrusts into the woman's chest, counting first to himself, then aloud. ". . .three. . .four. . .five. . ."

Briggs turned his attention toward the front door when he picked up the sound of a siren in the distance. "I'll make sure they know where we are," he said, then he ran out onto the front lawn, waving his arms.

"One. . .two. . .three. . .four. . .five. . ." Whitloe tried again. "Come on, Geneva. Gladys'll never let me hear the end of it if I let you go. One. . .two. . .three. . ."

Geneva Graham Todd made one final grimace then her head turned limply to one side.

Hunter kept on pumping until the coroner arrived.

Chapter Eight

"Post" Mortems

TOO CLOSE.

That was entirely too damn close.

A hand, shaking more with excitement than with fear, moved a pen across a notepad, over and over and over. Lips curled back to reveal clenched teeth, a horrific smile.

Four, so far. That was four. But I must be careful. That was too close, and work isn't done yet.

The tip of the ballpoint wore into the page. Redoubled, retripled lines weakened the fibers with slowly drying ink. The sheet began to tear. Reddened eyes darted from the paper, to the small box, and back again. The hand copied an image, running in a series of arcs and curves.

Over and over and over.

Friday would bring number five. And the beginning of the second phase.

Sweat matted the brow. The smile broadened a little.

Over and. . .

For another countless time, the hand circled, completing once again the cursive, capital letter "G."

It was all working so perfectly.
The throat choked back a laugh.
What a hell of a comeback this would be.

***

"It's ten-thirty," noted someone from the News Desk. "Has anyone heard from Charlotte yet?"

"Keep your shorts on," she called, entering the door behind him. "Here I am. My fucking car dumped all its oil, and the engine seized on the way in." She brushed absently at a small grease stain on the hem of her dress. "Great. This thing's ruined."

Otto Nicholson walked over to her and said, "I know the name of a great mechanic, if you need it."

A bit frustrated, she dropped the edge of her dress and waved him on. "No thanks. I'm junking that piece of shit. It's about time I treated myself to a new car anyway." She made contact with the reporter who had asked where she had been. "Abernathy. What's on your mind?" she asked, and she led him into her office. "Paul," she said to me, "how about getting us some coffee."

***

Captain Atherton had corralled Hunter Whitloe and Jonathan Briggs the moment they had returned from the coroner's office where they had left Geneva Todd's body.

"Just what the fuck is going on here, Hunter?" he raved at the detective. "No, no," he said before the man could respond, "let me see if I have it right. We've got another dead body, and still no clue as to who is doing this."

"In the Lieutenant's defense," Briggs said, "we really can't be sure if this one was the work of our serial killer. Sure, the woman's dead, but it looks like an apparent heart attack, sir. We didn't find her choked on any cereal, like we found the others."

"But the cereal *was* there, wasn't it, Hunter?" Atherton asked.

"Yes, sir. My guess is we got there before the perp could follow through with his little breakfast scenario. The table was set. There were Golden Grahams in the bowl." He took a moment to explain the connection between the cereal brand and the deceased.

"Let's just run with the assumption that this *is* our lunatic's handiwork, shall we?" said the Captain. "No other person has popped up dead this morning, unless you know something I don't."

"No, sir," Whitloe said. "She's the only one."

"And today was the day we were expecting it," Atherton said. "If we continue with Briggs's postal delivery theory."

The deputy straightened up a bit at the mention of his name with the one thing that appeared to have been guessed correctly so far. He fought hard not to smile too broadly.

"Don't look so smug, Deputy," the Captain warned him. "That little success of yours didn't help stop this morning's murder, did it?"

"No, sir," Briggs replied, looking down at the floor, beaten.

"Well then," Atherton continued. "Just what the hell are we going to do now?" The Captain looked up when he heard the knock on his office door. "Who is it?"

Probation Officer Birdie Burton cracked the door slowly, sticking her head in with a bit of caution. "Pardon me, sir. But the mail just came in, and I thought you'd want to see this as soon as possible."

Hunter Whitloe pivoted to see what she had brought with her, but he didn't really have to look to know what to expect.

In her hand, she held the fifth 3" x 4" x 1-1/2" brown-wrapped package.

Within moments, their four sets of eyes pondered the single-serving sized box of Post Raisin Bran sitting on the Captain's blotter.

"Well," noted Atherton, "this seems to blow your General Mills theory. This is an entirely different cereal company altogether."

Silently, Deputy Briggs was rejoicing.

"Not necessarily," Burton said. "Maybe this switch in brands is intentional. Maybe 'Post' is the clue."

"Or maybe the guy's just slipping," Whitloe added. "He could be getting sloppy. He's been moving too fast not to have made some mistakes."

"And it's those mistakes that'll lead us right to him," Atherton said. "Hunter, you said you thought you heard the back door slam at Geneva Todd's place. Maybe we are getting close. Closer than he would like. And this," he said, pointing to the small cereal box, "is meant to throw us off a little."

"If you'll pardon my saying so, sir," Burton said, "the Lieutenant's timing this morning couldn't be related to this change in cereal makers."

"How do you figure?" the Captain asked.

"Yeah," Whitloe chimed in, trying not to feel insulted.

"Well, if Briggs's mail delivery theory is correct," she explained, "he'd have to have mailed this thing *yesterday*. There's no way he would have known that the Lieutenant would have come so close to catching him this morning."

"She's got a point," Briggs said, sending a smile her way.

"So then," the Captain surmised, "this change from General Mills to Post could mean something entirely different."

"Or nothing at all," she said, expressing their worst fear.

"What else do we have to go on?" Atherton asked. "What else are we missing here?"

"We still have that Tony Tyger connection," Whitloe said. "He's still on the loose, and I did find a copy of the *Times* on the Todd's doorstep."

"Good," the Captain said. "Hunter, I want you to double your efforts in finding that boy." He gave a closer look at the box of Raisin Bran. "Now, let's assume that the General Mills thing meant something, and this 'Post' here is a second in a series of clues."

"Well," noted Briggs, "we can pretty much rule out the disgruntled worker or angry consumer theory. Maybe the 'General Mills' itself is important. Do we have any whacked-out military veterans in Chestnut Grove?"

Whitloe snorted. "Maybe we'll find what we're looking for under the town wind*mill*," he said. "Before you get all excited, Briggs, there isn't one of those either."

"Hunter, stop the bickering," Atherton said. "I like his creative thinking. Briggs, you should keep on that list of General Mills distributors. There must be something there. If you come up with some tie to this 'Post' number, let me know."

"Yes, sir," the deputy replied, burdened once again.

"Hunter, be sure to get back with the coroner's office today, and see if they're able to link this morning's body with the other three."

Ten-to-one she's got elevated nicotine levels in her, Whitloe thought. "Yes, sir," he said.

"Burton," the Captain said, "I want you to get over to the *Times* and obtain a printout of anyone who gets home delivery of the morning edition in Chestnut Grove. Maybe there's something there we've overlooked."

"Just steer clear of a Charlotte Journigan," Whitloe warned. "She's a particularly nosy news editor, simply looking for a story. I was at the morgue when she called down there yesterday for some inside information."

"She didn't get any, I hope," Atherton said.

"No chance," Whitloe assured him. "They're on our side."

"Good, because right now, we can use all the help we can get."

***

I was pouring over my background info on Black and Pirelli, along with my limited research on Totah when Charlotte called for me.

"Blazer!" she shouted from inside the confines of her office.

"What's up, Chie—, I mean, Charlotte," I said as I stepped inside.

"Have a seat," she instructed. She fired up another cigarette, indicating the chair in front of her desk with the hand holding the lighter. "First, I wanted to apologize for coming down on you as hard as I did last week."

"You don't have. . ."

"Let me finish," she interrupted, exhaling smoke as she spoke. "I've got a tight ship to run here, and I can't have anything going on without my knowledge or approval. You see where I'm coming from?"

I paled. *Did she know that I was following up on those three recent deaths? If so, how*? I tried not to look nervous.

"Anyway, with that all said, I wanted to let you know that I'm willing to give you another try." She reached for a small note that Abernathy had brought from the News Desk before I came in. She handed it to me, continuing with, "One of our city's more beloved public librarians — correct that, *former* librarians — died this morning. Heart attack. There was a fair bit of commotion at her home this morning, and we picked up the tip on our scanner."

With a glance to her note, I read the basics: Geneva Todd, 71, retired librarian for Contra Costa County until 1990, former spouse of Spencer Graham (deceased 1991), survived by husband Clyde Arthur Todd. . .

"I'd like a sidebar like the one you did on Matthew Black," she said. "Detailed, thoughtful. . .a tribute to her work and standing in the community. It'll run in the afternoon and tomorrow morning's editions. You know the bit."

While I was happy to see that Charlotte was giving me a shot at getting back into her good graces, I quietly felt a bit anxious. Actually, I was getting used to her ignoring me. It had given me all that free time to dig up what I had on Black, Pirelli, and now Totah. Research on this routine passing would take up all afternoon. I wouldn't be able to make any progress on the real story I was working on, the one she *didn't* know about.

"Sure. You got it," I said, trying to sound appreciative. "I'll get started right away."

"Oh, Paul," she said as I got up to leave. "If you get stuck or have any questions, I want you coming directly to me. Understand?"

"Sure. And thanks for giving me a second chance."

Stepping through her door, I found myself cursing my subservience as well as the bad timing of it all until I caught sight of a uniformed police officer leaving the Circulation department with a small stack of papers under her arm. I passed by my desk and deposited the copy of Charlotte's assignment, retrieving a blank notepad in the process.

"Another assignment?" Otto asked as I passed.

"Yeah," I said absently, my attention focused on Circulation and the departing officer. "Some dead librarian. For this afternoon's edition."

"Good for you," he said, returning to his own work.

I reached the Circulation desk shortly after the woman in uniform had slipped out the front door. "Blazer," I said, introducing myself to an unfamiliar face behind the counter. "Paul Blazer. News and obituaries." I extended a hand.

Shaking it, the older man replied, "Millhouse. Circulation. What can I do for you?"

"That female officer who just left," I said, with slight indication to the front door, "what did she want?" I hoped I wasn't being too blunt.

Millhouse smiled. "Oh, just a printout of all our subscribers to the morning edition. Said she needed it for a fundraiser the department was doing. They wanted to canvas as many areas as possible, and they thought our records would help."

That's strange, I thought, but I tried not to let on. "Can you give me a copy of everything you gave her?" I asked. "I'm doing a little canvassing of my own."

Millhouse gave me a skeptical look but then said, "Oh, what the hell. You work here, right? What harm could that do?" He turned to a computer, pressed a button, and readied his printer. Within moments, the machine was typing name after name and easing them out on sprocketed paper through a slot in the top. When it had finished, he tore off the last sheet and folded the information into a neat stack, handing it to me. "Just don't go selling this to some direct mail marketing group, or it'll be both our butts."

"Not to worry," I said, thanking him with a nod and a smile before going back to my desk to research my "real" assignment.

***

"This one used clip-ons, Toe," medical examiner Redford Malone said, indicating the lack of pierce holes in Geneva Graham Todd's earlobes. "You think you can handle this one without me for a while?"

"What's the matter, Malone?" Tess Taggert asked. She kept most of her attention on the scalpel she was sharpening rather than her partner as she spoke. "The job getting to you?"

Malone took off his white lab coat, hooking it on the coat rack near the door. "You know," he said, "I thought I was leaving most of this behind when I moved from Fresno. Don't get me wrong. I like the work, and we don't get a quarter of the stiffs my old job did. But I hope this," with a gesture to the body on the examination table, "isn't any indication where this town's headed. It didn't take too much for Fresno to become the Murder Capital of California, you know."

Picking up another metal instrument, Taggert gave Malone a sympathetic grin and nodded toward the door. "Go ahead, cue ball. Go grab some lunch or something. I can hold down the fort for a while."

"Thanks. I'll be back in a couple of hours."

"Take as long as you need," she said.

He made his way to the white LeBaron he had parked in the lot. Its bumper sticker read: "FRESNO — It isn't the end of the world, but you can see it from here." As he unlocked the driver's side door, Hunter Whitloe pulled up alongside in his patrol car.

"Is the doc still here?" Whitloe asked, meaning Taggert.

"Yeah," Malone replied with little enthusiasm. "She's in with the one you brought in this morning." He said nothing else as he climbed in his car, closed the door, and drove away.

The detective went inside, and a moment later, he was poking his head into the autopsy room.

"I saw your partner as I pulled in," he said to Taggert. "Is he all right?"

"He's fine. It's just getting to be a little too much for him right now."

Whitloe moved next to the still form of Geneva Todd. "I think I know how he feels."

Just then, the telephone rang, and Taggert answered it before it could ring twice. "Taggert here. . .Uh-huh. . .Thanks, Michael. You do great work. I'll look for it on the fax." Hanging up, she turned to Whitloe and said, "That blood sample I drew this morning at the scene? We've got preliminary toxicologicals already."

"That's fast," Whitloe said. "Can they speed the rest of them up, too?"

"Don't count on it," she said, leading him to the fax machine, which just began to pick up. "I had to promise the guy a date to get this." They both watched as the cover sheet came, followed by the second page with the results. Taggert picked it up and scanned it quickly. "It goes a lot faster when you have them screen for a specific substance," she said.

"Nicotine," the detective said.

"That's right," she said, turning the sheet toward him to see. "But you're not going to like this."

He took the page from her, bringing it closer, hoping he had misread what he just saw. "Negative," he said.

"Right again. Not a trace."

"How can that be?" he asked.

She took a step back to the body, saying, "Well, let's see if we can find out, shall we?"

Probation Officer Burton caught up with Deputy Jonathan Briggs at a mom-and-pop convenience store on the corner of Hickory and Fourth Streets shortly after eleven fifteen.

"Any luck so far?" she said, coming up behind him as he walked down the dry cereal aisle. She had her printout of morning newspaper subscribers in a folder under her right arm.

"Not really," he said. "But look at this." Pointing to the rows of breakfast foods he read them off to her, one at a time. "Berry Berry Kix. . .Cocoa Puffs. . .Fiber One. . .Cinnamon Toast Crunch. Here." He stopped in front of the next box and asked, "What's wrong with this picture?"

"Total Raisin Bran," Burton read. "What? I don't get it."

"Look who makes it," he said.

She looked to the upper left-hand corner of the box and, spying the large, cursive capital "G," she said, "General Mills." She considered it for a moment then said, "I still don't get it."

"How about this one?" Briggs tried. He now raised a hand to the box of Raisin Nut Bran, also by General Mills.

"Sorry, Briggs. What do you see?"

"That General Mills has at least *two* raisin bran-type cereals," he explained. "If our guy wanted to keep it all consistent, with the same company, he could have. Easily."

"So you think that 'Post' *is* the next clue."

"Kinda makes sense, doesn't it?" he reasoned.

"We're talking about a possible serial killer here, Jon. One with a pretty warped M.O. How do you expect it all to make sense?"

"From what I've read about serial killers, they stick to some very consistent patterns. Some have very similar victims. Some kill during the same time of the month. . ."

"But with the *cereal* being the bottom line in these cases," she said, "the manufacturer may have just been a coincidence."

"I don't buy it," the deputy noted. "This guy's been fairly meticulous. Remember the breakfast get-up at Pirelli's place? I don't think that he would have changed to another cereal manufacturer unless it was for a reason."

Birdie Burton finally gave in. "I see your point," she said. "Say, why don't we take a break from your list, get some lunch, and go over the names I picked up at the newspaper? That's another consistency in all of this we still have to figure out."

"You're on," he said. "I'm buying."

"Jonnie," she said with a lift in her voice, "is this a date?"

The deputy felt himself blush, and he turned away to hide his smile. "Come on," he said. "How's Chinese sound?"

By the end of that afternoon, Hunter Whitloe had seen more of the late Geneva Graham Todd than he had seen when she had been alive. She *was* quiet though.

"Looks like it all came down to this," Tess Taggert said, reexamining the heart and pacemaker she had removed earlier. She took the mechanical device and gave it a firm whack against the counter. "Pacemaker stopped dead. And she soon followed."

"Come on, doc. Are you telling me that she *wasn't* knocked off by our serial killer?"

"I'm not saying that at all," the coroner replied. "Remember this?" she asked, gesturing to the small, reddish welt in the center of the woman's back.

"It's a mark like we found on Pirelli," Whitloe said.

"And Matthew Black," she added. She looked over the case files from the three other victims. "So, it's not an irritation from the patch. We've got no nicotine in her."

"Like we have in the others," the detective said.

"It's not a bruise or contusion, as if she'd been struck."

Whitloe thought for a moment. "What would have her pacemaker seize up like that? Her microwave?" He remembered having seen a large one in her kitchen.

"I've heard of cases," she said, "but that won't explain the marks on the bodies. It'd have to be some sort of direct contact."

"How about a cattle prod?" Whitloe said, wondering how far-fetched this whole thing would get.

"That's it!" Taggert cried.

"A cattle prod?!"

She laughed a bit. "Something like it, I'd say. Like a stun gun. You know, those things bought for self-protection."

Whitloe shook his head. "It'd have to be pretty powerful to leave a welt like that."

"Oh, I don't know, Hunter," the coroner said. "I'm no expert. Maybe it's been modified somehow. But if it were some kind of incapacitating weapon, it would help explain a lot of things."

"Like why there never appears to have been much of a struggle."

"For starters. If this guy — or gal, come to think of it — zaps them first, he could do anything he wanted to them. They're down on the ground semiconscious. Not much of a struggle there."

Whitloe watched as his number of suspects just expanded to include both genders. "So the guy we're after could be a woman," he said.

"Don't tell me you haven't considered it," Taggert said. "Jeez, what a chauvinist!"

"Well, I. . ."

"Look. More women tend to buy those kinds of things. And wouldn't you be more likely to invite a strange *woman* into your home than a strange *man*? You *did* say there haven't been any signs of forced entry at any of the crime scenes," she reminded him. "If you ask me, I'd say you've got a whole new tunnel to go down, my friend."

And it's probably long, dark, and with a couple of guys with baseball bats at the end of it, Whitloe thought. Or at the least, a hand-held stun gun and a bowl of Post Raisin Bran.

"Well, I'm sorry this didn't seem to answer too many of your questions, Hunter," she said. "But I'm glad it helped out with some of mine." Picking up a pen, she began to make a number of notes in each of her four case files.

"Great," Whitloe said, leaving. "A shit-load of more things to look into, and I still only have until Friday morning."

As the door shut, he didn't hear Toe Tag Taggert's final comment: "It kind of gives a whole new meaning to the word 'deadline,' doesn't it?" She turned back to the body on the slab, laughing.

***

My sidebar on the deceased librarian made it to the afternoon edition with the usual amount of red marks I'd come to expect from Assistant News Editor Charlotte Journigan. Writing and rewriting it also managed to consume the better part of the afternoon, something else I kind of expected, so when five rolled around, I found myself leaving for home with my stack of notes on Black, Totah, and Pirelli. I'd have to review them on my own time, if I wanted to look at them at all.

"*Guten tag*," I said to Dante as I opened the door with my free hand. "*Ich bin zu Hause*."

Catching me off guard, the dog ran past me, barking happily. Then he haunched down on his front legs, growling playfully, before circling my legs three times and bolting away toward the street. Within seconds, he had disappeared from view.

"Dante, no! Come back here!"

Next came a sudden squealing of tires, a thud, and a yelp that I knew could have only had one source.

"Dante!"

I dropped the keys I held in one hand and the notes from the paper in the other and rounded the shrubbery that lined the yard in time to watch an old, brown Monte Carlo speed out of sight.

"Dante," I called again, unable to locate him in that instant. A beat later, however, I found him. He half ran, half limped toward me, eyes wide with terror and tongue hanging out of the side of his mouth. He bled from the nose, which bubbled and frothed as he panted wildly. Breaking into a run, I met him halfway, at the edge of the lot. I crouched down to see a few of his teeth were missing, and his gums bled as well. He had pulled his right front paw to his chest and tried to stay standing as best he could.

"It's okay, Dante," I soothed in hushed tones. "It's okay." I stroked the top of his head to try to calm him, and at that moment, shock gripped him, and he lost bowel control.

Scooping him up, I jogged back to the house and got us both inside. I pulled the blanket from my futon, wrapped him in it, then picked up the phone.

"Damn," I said, realizing that it was after regular vet hours, and no one at Dr. Grimma's would pick up. Instinctively, I stabbed 911.

"Nine-one-one emergency," came a female voice. "Is this a medical emergency?"

I fumbled. "I guess so," I said. "Look, I don't need an ambulance or anything. My dog's just been hit by a car, and his vet's office is closed. Do you have any idea where I can take him?"

"One moment please," she said, and half a minute later, she read the address and phone number of an after-hours veterinary clinic that could see him.

"Thanks," I said. "Thanks a lot."

After a quick call to the emergency vet, I loaded the dog into my Jeep and sped down the street. By this time, Dante had gotten pretty quiet, and his eyes had taken on a fixed stare. Blood seeped from his nose and mouth and pooled on my front seat, winding its way down to the carpet.

"Hang in there, mutt," I said with a brush of his ear. "We're almost there."

It was another couple of hours before I saw my dog again, resting under anesthetic after a quick surgery.

"He's a lucky dog, Mr. Blazer," the attending vet, Dr. Joan Benton, said. "Most big dogs like him that get hit by cars usually have a lot of broken bones, sometimes a crushed rib cage, since that's one of the largest parts making contact. Dante looks like he just took a knock to the head, probably with the bumper. I doubt he'd have been as lucky if he had made it under the car."

"He's going to be all right then?" I asked, the worried parent.

"We'd like to keep him for a few days observation, but I don't foresee any complications. You can pick him up on Friday. How's that?"

I reached for my wallet and a credit card. "That'll be okay, I guess." I looked at my dog, bandaged and bruised, but sleeping for the moment. I carefully brushed the back of his neck, and said, "See you Friday, pal." Making it to the reception area, I paid the clerk and began to calm down as I climbed into my Jeep and headed home.

For the rest of that evening and over the next day and a half, I went over my background information on Matthew Black, Terry Totah, and Nicholas Pirelli, searching for some bit of evidence that would prove that their deaths were somehow related. Things at the *Times* were relatively quiet, so I had an opportunity to dig a little more on the late fitness instructor, too. All I came across, however, was a half-page feature in the Entertainment section three years ago, announcing his foray into the world of public access TV with his morning exercise show, "Total Fitness with Terry Totah."

Hardly a scandal, as the articles on Black and Pirelli had been.

Cross referencing the names with the list of morning edition subscribers, I found that only Black and Totah routinely received the paper. Pirelli's subscription had been some kind of mistake, of course, as I recalled the nasty phone complaint he registered with Cindi Bates on the Tuesday prior to his death. Charlotte had intercepted the call, referring to him as a "syphilitic whore-monger" when he tried to get out of line with her.

All three had died in the morning. That much was consistent. But it wasn't enough to push an article linking them together past my hard-nosed news editor.

There was that thing with Artie Kellogg, the police protection, and the Trix, but at this point in time, I couldn't see anything solid there either. It was just weird.

Then, around three-thirty Thursday afternoon, a call came through to my desk that had a lot of things fall into place.

"Paul Blazer," I said, answering line two.

"Mr. Blazer, it's Shannon McMillan of Chestnut Grove Public Access TV. I produced Terry Totah's fitness show, until, like he *died*, that is."

***

By Thursday afternoon, Lieutenant Detective Hunter Whitloe was running out of options.

The local gun shop — the only store that sold hand-held stun guns — didn't keep records of who had purchased them, and the proprietor was an aging, deaf codger who had a hard enough time remembering the detective's name as they spoke, let alone recalling who might have been in the store looking for self-protection devices in the last few weeks.

With the help of Briggs and Burton, he reviewed the morning newspaper circulation roster, but it failed to yield a single subscriber with the last name of "Post," or with the more unlikely "Raisin" or "Bran." (In an act of sheer desperation, they checked those names, too.)

Briggs had suggested that the latest clue could be a reference to some member of the local postal service, but when they followed through with every employee of the town's two post offices, not one of them received the morning edition of the *Times*.

No one in Chestnut Grove boasted to be a member of the California Raisin Advisory Board, past, present, or future. Not one of the local bands planned on doing a remake of Marvin Gaye's classic, "I Heard It Through the Grapevine." (And most of the members guffawed at the mere mention of the idea, a reaction that amused Hunter Whitloe in no way, shape, or form.)

It was only by accident that the detective finally met up with the elusive Antonio Tyger. He saw the kid bolt when he was showing a picture of the lad to a girl behind the counter at a Burger King.

"Freeze!" he yelled after the kid, and freeze he did.

When taken downtown for questioning, however, he denied any knowledge of the cereal murders, but was quick to acknowledge who had pulled the trigger on Deputy Samuels.

It had been his older brother, Charles, who had been growing pot in a closet in the house. Figuring that the place was being raided, Charles had his parents — under duress — gut out the thriving crop of marijuana plants and hightail it out the back of the house. He stayed long enough to pump a few rounds through the front door. They all had been hiding at a sister's in neighboring Antioch, and after a few phone calls, Whitloe had half a dozen squad cars surround the place and capture the trio without incident.

And *no*, the kid didn't go by the name "Tony."

With less than twenty-four hours to go before he expected to find another dead body, Whitloe faced the realization that this joker was probably going to get away with it again.

But the fact that there had to be something else he was overlooking, another piece to this crazy puzzle that would blow it all wide open, still nagged away at him, and of course, it wouldn't let him sleep.

***

"Well, don't you look like you just won the lottery," Otto Nicholson said to me as I hung up the phone with Shannon McMillan. "What's up?"

I was smiling so hard my face hurt. Getting up with my notes on the three dead men, I said, "You know the recent articles we've run on Matthew Black, Terry Totah, and Nicholas Pirelli?"

"Black, Totah, and. . ." Otto repeated, looking lost.

"Pirelli," I said quickly. "The three dead guys."

"Oh, yes. Wha—"

"I think I've just come across something that ties them all together," I said.

"'Together'?" he repeated.

"That's what I said. I think they all were *murdered.* Come on. I have to run this by Charlotte."

Moments later, Otto and I stood in front of the Assistant News Editor's desk, and I was babbling like a crazy man.

"Let me see if I have this right," Charlotte said calmly, interrupting me. "Black, Totah, *and* Pirelli were all. . ."

"Murdered," I said again. "I just got through talking with Shannon McMillan, producer of 'Total Fitness with Terry Totah,' and he confirmed that they found Total cereal all over the place. Matthew Black died face first in a bowl of Wheaties, and I happen to know that Pirelli was found in bed, lying in a bunch of Trix."

"A *cereal* killer," Otto interjected.

"I know it sounds crazy," I admitted, "but it's a little too bizarre to be just a coincidence."

Charlotte glared at me. "I understand your tip from this McMillan character, and we all knew how they found Matthew Black. Ironic as all hell, I have to admit." She took a thoughtful drag from her cigarette, then drowned it in her ashtray with a hiss. "And I'm not sure I want to know how you got the Trix tidbit about Pirelli. . ."

"A reporter doesn't always have to reveal his sources," Otto said, speaking up in my defense.

"Still," she said, "how much of this correlation — aside from the cereal — can we actually confirm? We can't go off and write something like this without covering our own asses."

"You and I both know that the police aren't talking," I said.

"And you wouldn't really expect them to," Otto offered, "if they've got three dead bodies found under similar and suspicious circumstances, with no idea how they got that way."

"Granted," Charlotte said. "I can always try again with the coroner's office." She picked up her phone and rang an in-house line. I could hear a phone ring on one of the desks out in the news room, then she said, "Abernathy, get in here. I've got something I'd like you to. . ."

Before I caught myself thinking, I slammed my finger on the cradle, disconnecting her. "Oh, no you don't," I said, and with another movement, I closed her office door in the face of the more-seasoned reporter as he approached. "I haven't busted my butt to get this far, then have you reassign it to someone else. This one's mine."

Abernathy knocked on the door behind me. "Charlotte? Is everything okay?"

The Assistant News Editor delivered a look that told me my career in the newspaper business was finished. "Never mind, Abernathy," she said at last. "I was wrong. Things are covered already."

Within a few seconds, I could hear the reporter retreat back to his desk, and I was able to redirect all my attention on Charlotte and what she was about to say next.

"You've got a pair of big ones, Blazer. You surprise me."

"To say the least," Otto agreed.

"So this one is mine," I pressed. "I get to write it."

"Not so fast, hot shot," she said. "There's still a lot of this theory of yours I'd like confirmed before we hit Page One."

"More than a couple of things, I'd say," Nicholson said.

"I'll do whatever it takes," I said. "Just give me first crack at it, okay?"

"Let's first see what we can get from the coroner's office," she said, picking up the phone again. "After that, you report directly to me with anything else that comes up. Nicholson, back him up." She shot back at me. "You're still too green to fly solo."

"I understand."

Next, she spoke into the phone. "Yeah, is Redford Malone there. . .I'll hold. . ."

"This could be your big break, kid," Nicholson whispered to me. "Good work."

"Malone," she continued, "Journigan. Now don't give me any shit this time. We know that we've got some psycho running around doing funny things with breakfast cereal and a few of Chestnut Grove's prominent citizens. Three, to be exact. So if you don't want your bald little head plastered across the front page from here until Tuesday, you'll tell us whatever we want to know. Got it? Ah. . .that's better." She flashed a smile and sent a wink my way. "How 'bout I send one of my men over to speak with you personally. Uh-huh. . .sure. . .Tomorrow's fine. Say nine o'clock? Uh-huh. That'll give you a couple of hours to get situated and decide just what exactly you're going to say. Not that you'd ever hold anything back, eh? Good. You're a stand-up guy, Malone. We'll be in touch." Hanging up, she said, "It's all set. Nicholson, get the man the address out of the news desk's Rolodex, will you?"

Otto left, leaving Charlotte to consider me once again. At last, she said, "I'm taking a big risk with you, Blazer. I wasn't kidding when I said I want you to check in with me every step of the way. If I get the feeling you're fucking this up, I'll yank you from it so fast you won't know what happened. I'll have your job, your career, and your head as well. Got it?"

I was flying so high at the moment that her threat didn't even phase me. "Got it, Chief," I said.

Charlotte Journigan gave me a look, but didn't reprimand me this time. Lighting up another cigarette, she shooed me out. "Be sure to go over your notes again before your interview with Malone tomorrow, and see me first thing when you come back."

"Tomorrow," I said, then I was gone.

"Dr. Taggert isn't in yet," the receptionist said when I arrived at the coroner's office promptly at nine Friday morning.

"I'm here to see a Redford Malone, actually," I said, running a hand through my flattop and straightening my tie. I was so keyed up for this that I hadn't been able to sleep much last night. I hope it didn't show.

"Oh," she said. "Dr. Malone's been here since seven, I think. Before I got here. His office is down the hall, to the left. If he's not there, he may be in the main autopsy room. We've been kind of busy lately."

"So I understand," I said. "Thank you."

Walking down the hall, I gave my microcassette recorder one final check. Okay, that's working. I felt for the official "PRESS" pass I had picked up at the office before I left yesterday. Uh-huh. Got that, too.

I stopped in front of the door marked "REDFORD MALONE, Deputy Coroner" and gave it a firm knock. After half a minute and no answer, I tried again before turning the knob and looking inside.

"Lights are on," I said, panning the room, "but nobody's home."

A little shudder ran through me as I continued down to the main autopsy room. It was quiet and cold, and I could hear my footsteps echo as I walked. I hadn't seen a dead body since my grandmother's open casket service. If Dr. Malone was working, I wasn't sure just what I'd see when I walked in.

This time I decided not to knock, and I pulled open the door and confidently strode in.

Crunch, crunch, crunch, crunch.

My eyes shot downward, and I found myself standing in a puddle of milk and cereal.

Post Raisin Bran, to be exact.

I could tell from the overturned box at the foot of the autopsy slab on which the body of Deputy Coroner Redford Malone lay. On an instrument tray beside him was a glass of orange juice, a half-empty bowl, and a couple of slices of toast. From the looks of it, he appeared to be gagged with a mouthful of the raisins and bran flakes. I didn't hang around much longer before I backed out of the room and yelled, "Somebody call 911. There's a dead man in here!"

The receptionist gave a little laugh until she realized I wasn't referring to the standard "dead man" variety one would expect in such a place. A beat later, she was on the phone.

Chapter Nine

Captain's Crunch

HUNTER WHITLOE ARRIVED ON scene within fifteen minutes, with Briggs, Burton, and two other officers in tow. They carried all the necessary evidence kits, collection bags, and camera equipment for the job, and one of the men started roping off the area with yellow tape marked "POLICE LINE — Do Not Cross."

As the pair of Briggs and Burton stepped into the autopsy room to do a preliminary walk-through and make sketches of the body, the detective cornered the receptionist and asked, "So, who found him?"

"Uh, that would be me," I said, standing from a chair some ten feet behind him. Turning, he faced me, and when his expression changed an instant later, I knew he remembered where he had met me before.

Lieutenant Detective Hunter Whitloe had been the lead investigator in that previous Chestnut Grove murder case where I'd been considered the prime suspect, more than a year and a half ago. It was Whitloe's narrow-minded follow-up that made my life, and the life of my friend Dominic, a nightmare as he asked some rather embarrassing questions and relayed some very private facts to our friends, family members, and co-workers throughout the town. In essence, his "evidence" had me sit six months in the Martinez Detention Facility, to endure a farce of a trial that ended in my acquittal.

Not to mention his own public, professional embarrassment.

"You," was all he said.

Extending a hand, I stepped forward and said, "Yes, it's me. Paul Blazer, if you don't remember. I can't say that it's a pleasure to see you again, Lieutenant."

Whitloe made a conscious effort to pull back his arm, refusing my gesture for the moment. Instead, he retrieved a notepad and pen from his back pocket. "Blazer," he said, writing. "Do you mind telling me just what the hell you're doing here in the coroner's office? Don't you have a class to teach or something?"

I gave him a look. Of course he didn't know. "I work for the *Times* now. News room. I gave up teaching high school shortly after we last saw one another. It seems that the conservative residents of Chestnut Grove had a hard time accepting a gay teacher in their public schools."

"Understandable," Whitloe snapped back. He continued writing, saying, "And you're here today because. . ."

"I had an appointment with the deceased, Dr. Malone," I said. "*Before* he was deceased," I added quickly, not wanting to give the man any ideas. "My editor had arranged it yesterday. We were going to discuss the strange circumstances involved in the deaths of Matthew Black, Terry Totah, and former councilman Nicholas Pirelli. We have reason to believe that they were all murdered." To counter the detective, I reached for my microcassette recorder and turned it on, just under his chin. "Maybe you'd like to make a statement about it."

Twisting away, Whitloe demanded, "Turn that thing off. No comment. I repeat, 'No comment.'"

I complied for the moment but said, "Ah, come on, Lieutenant. We both know something really twisted is going on. What do you say we compare notes?"

"'Notes'?" he repeated, looking interested.

"Yeah," I said. "I've got a ton of information on all three of them that had me suspect that their deaths were somehow related. I'd be happy to share it with you for the inside scoop on what you've been up to all this time."

"Out of the question," Whitloe said firmly.

"Look. Whatever you know isn't the whole picture, or we wouldn't have a dead coroner in the next room, right? Just tell me what you know, and maybe we can solve this thing."

To that, Hunter Whitloe did not respond.

Taking it as a sign, I decided to push a little further. "Together," I said.

He shot me a look that told me that "together" was the most uncomfortable part of all of this for him.

I smiled. "Now," I said, "just what is it with all this cereal?"

After Deputy Coroner Tess Taggert showed up and agreed to supervise Whitloe's four co-workers in collecting evidence, the detective accompanied me back to the *Times* office. I immediately introduced him to Charlotte Journigan, and in the privacy of her office, we told her of the death of Redford Malone.

"You found him like all the others?" she asked, avoiding any emotion by getting right down to business.

"Yep," I said. "This time it was Post Raisin Bran."

She strained a little laugh at that. "Makes sense," she said. A questioning look from Whitloe had her explain. "'Post.' As in *post mortem.* He was a coroner, after all. And he hailed from Fresno, the Raisin Capital of California. I'd say this killer of yours has a very warped sense of humor, Lieutenant."

"Tell me about it," Whitloe replied.

"The Lieutenant's been getting a small box of each cereal a few days prior to the murders," I said, relaying what little the detective had already told me. "As a clue of some sort."

"So," Charlotte said, "You got a box of Wheaties before you found Matthew Black, Total prior to Totah. . ."

"Yeah," Whitloe interrupted. I could see that he was beginning to get a little impatient. "Like that. Now, what have you got?" he asked. "I want to catch this bastard."

Pulling out my background research on Black, Totah, and Pirelli, I spread the articles over the top of Charlotte's desk. Both she and the detective seemed both surprised and intrigued at the amount of information I had, and they remained rapt as I went through it all one piece at a time.

"Matthew Black," I said, "a former Olympic hopeful, forced from the limelight and stripped of his product endorsements after the scandal that ensued following the discovery that he didn't like one of the items he promoted, namely Wheaties breakfast cereal."

Moving to my information on Pirelli, I continued, "I came across this on the former councilman next. He was forced from political office after he was found to have a fondness for prostitutes. . ."

"Trix," Charlotte said, understanding.

Whitloe shifted nervously, saying nothing.

"I backtracked to Totah after I got a call from his show's producer, Shannon McMillan." Sliding his article to the fore, I said, "He told me about finding the man with Total corn flakes everywhere. As you can see, I found something on him, too."

The detective scanned the article, then said, "But where's the scandal? This is a feature. It's in the Entertainment section, for chrissakes."

"True," I said. "I thought of that, and right now, it's something I can't explain. My guess on the selection of this particular cereal, however, is the similarity with his last name."

"The man had trouble pronouncing his *L*'s," Whitloe said. "He would've pronounced 'Total' as 'Totah.'"

"Interesting," said Charlotte.

"Aside from the cereal," I said, "they all had articles on them in the *Times*, scandal or not. That's what I found anyway. That's what had me come to you, Charlotte, and want to talk with the coroner's office. To see if there were any other similarities I couldn't find on my own."

"So, is there an article on Malone?" Whitloe asked.

I looked at him. "Well, there's one way to find out."

A few minutes later, the three of us circled around the microfilm machine in the newspaper morgue as I scrolled through a number of back issues.

"Was there anything interesting about him?" I asked. "Anything that would get him in the paper?"

Both of them were silent for a minute until Charlotte said, "If I remember correctly, there was some stink when the town hired him on. Some people complained that there wasn't enough money in the budget, and Chestnut Grove's crime rate was so low, that we didn't need him."

"When was that?" I asked.

"A couple of years ago," she said. "Wait. It was January or February 1990."

"How can you be so sure?" Whitloe asked.

"I remember because the *Times* ran a series of stories of the town facing the new decade. We called it, 'Chestnut Grove in the Nineties' or something. Look back then."

I threaded the appropriate reel, and a moment later, I found it.

"BUDGET BLUNDER," read the headline. "Does the city really need a second Medical Examiner?" asked the subhead. In the middle of the copy was a photo of the balding Redford Malone. Back then, he had some hair left. I hit the "PRINT" button, and the machine copied it for us.

Whitloe picked up the sheet as it came out the side. Pondering it for a bit, he then asked, "Would you have anything on a Geneva Todd? I mean, Graham."

I craned my head up toward him from where I sat. "The librarian?" I asked. "Sure. I wrote a sidebar on her after her death on Tuesday. Why?"

"Get it for me, will ya?" he said.

I got up, went out to my desk, and returned with the information I'd found. Handing it to Whitloe, I watched him for some visible response.

"This isn't it," he said. "This is just the usual stuff. There's more. She had a pacemaker put in back in the summer of 1990. The town got together and pitched in to cover the surgery."

Finding the right microfilm reel, I rolled to the summer of 1990.

"There it is," I said, landing on a piece titled, "HAVE A HEART — Locals rally to fund former librarian's pacemaker surgery."

"Print that, too. Will ya?" Whitloe asked. Half a minute later, he held that copy as well.

"What's with that one, Lieutenant?" I wondered.

"We found her with a bowl of Golden Grahams," he said. Handing me the article, he said, "See? Her former name was 'Graham.' Her first marriage lasted fifty years."

"Golden," I said.

Whitloe straightened up and said softly to himself something I guess he had been wrestling with for a while. "So she *was* one of his victims." He looked back at me, and speaking in a firmer tone said, "Try one more. Artie Kellogg. Recently out of high school. Convicted of DUI. He now does high school assemblies. He did one last Friday."

"Right," I said, eager to see how this one fit in. I reached for a stack of actual papers that sat to the right of the microfilm machine. "He's pretty recent, so he wouldn't be on film yet." Paging through last Friday's edition, I found nothing, but when I backed up two days before that, I located the bit that ran, announcing his upcoming talk at Marshall Clancy High. I handed it to Whitloe, and said, "But he's still alive. I just talked to him last Monday."

"You *have* been busy," Charlotte Journigan said, impressed.

"That's what bothers me with this little theory of yours," Whitloe said. "He had an article, too, but he didn't get it. We thought for a while he'd be the one to end up in Trix."

"I see," I said, understanding the kid's connection to that cereal brand. "Well, you got me there."

Charlotte leaned over and fingered through the drawer of microfilm reels. "How about the original article? The one that reported his DUI?"

We found it, a small inch-and-a-half bit buried in the section of local news for that time, and a moment later, we had a copy of that, too. Still, it told us nothing.

"Why not Kellogg?" wondered Charlotte aloud.

I took some time to go over all of the write-ups, from Matthew Black to Redford Malone. When I was through, I tried, "Well, with the exception of this little bit on Kellogg when he got his DUI, he's the only one who seems to be fairly recent. Everyone else's piece is much older."

"And much longer," Charlotte noted.

Taking another look at each story, something finally flashed on me. I made a frantic search through all of them again before I spoke.

"What?" asked Detective Whitloe. "What do you see?"

I flipped each article around, presenting them to him one at a time, again in the order of Black to Malone. "What do *you* see, Lieutenant? What is common to all of these pieces?"

Whitloe stared at each one intently, but I could tell what I'd discovered remained lost on him.

"The by-line," I said, helping him out. "Look at the name on each article."

Charlotte and Whitloe looked together, and at the same time, they said, "Garrison Fitzgerald." The detective flipped to another page and read, "Garrison Fitzgerald." Then another. "Garrison Fitzgerald."

"You'll find that he wrote all of those," I said as they went through the final few. "Every one *except* this one."

"The Kellogg piece," Whitloe breathed. He took that one as well and saw that it had been written by one of the newer reporters, Kent Abernathy.

"If you're wondering," I said, "the older DUI bit had no by-line. It pretty much was a blurb."

"Who was this Garrison Fitzgerald joker?" asked Whitloe.

Charlotte Journigan answered him. "Technically, he's the owner of the paper. It's practically run by an executive committee now. He set that up when he decided to start writing instead of managing. That was quite a while ago."

"Where is he now?" the detective pressed. He looked at me this time.

"Indefinite leave," I said. "From what I've heard anyway. Otto said something about his wife and daughter being killed in a car accident, and Fitzgerald taking time off to regroup. What do you know, Charlotte?"

Looking to her, Whitloe and I could see her getting a little uncomfortable. She fidgeted.

"Come on," the detective said. "Spill it."

She fidgeted a little before she began. "Garry won the Pulitzer about this time last year," she said. "He was always very successful, and that was one of his proudest times." She paused, drew in a breath, then continued. "On the night of his award ceremony, his wife, Elizabeth, and their four-month-old daughter, Tess, drove separately. They were running a little late, and they didn't want him to miss his big day.

"Well, on the way to the celebration, they got into an accident. It was raining, and the roads were such a mess. Anyway, Elizabeth and Tess were. . ."

"Killed," I said, filling in her sentence.

But Charlotte shook her head. "No," she said. "Well, yes. Tess died on impact, but Garry's wife, Elizabeth, hung on for a number of months. He tried his best to care for her, but one day last September it was over."

"Then he cracked up and went on 'indefinite leave' as you call it," Whitloe said.

Charlotte nodded. "He checked himself into a clinic in Napa for help."

"I'll be sure to check and see if he's still there," Whitloe said.

"But why would Garry be doing something like this?" she asked.

"Well," I offered, "all of the people killed have been subjects of his articles. Maybe it's some way of striking back at the thing that he sees took his family away."

"But he was getting better," she said.

Whitloe looked at her.

"How do you know that, Charlotte?" I asked.

"Well, he'd write to me," she explained. Her eyes widened a bit. "Wait a minute. I'll show you." She left, and a little while later, she returned with a hand-written note and an envelope postmarked in Napa. Handing them to Whitloe, she said, "See? He says his doctors say he's making fine progress."

Whitloe examined the envelope. "It's dated January 8th. About two months ago. Nothing since?"

"Why, no," she replied.

He read over the hand-written note then turned it back around to her, pointing. "What the hell is this?" he asked. His finger rested on the capital, cursive "G" at the bottom.

"It's a 'G,'" she said. "For Garry. That's how he signed all of his things. Even the articles he'd do for the paper."

"That does it," Whitloe blurted. "I've got to make a call."

Just then a knock came at the door, and Otto Nicholson eased his head inside. "Excuse me," he said. "Are you Lieutenant Whitloe?"

"Yes. What is it?"

"There's a call for you from a Captain Atherton. Line three."

Whitloe stormed out of the newspaper morgue, following Otto to his desk. Punching the illuminated button at the base of the telephone, he brought the receiver to his ear. "Whitloe here. Uh-huh. . ." He snapped his fingers and made a gesture for a pen and a piece of paper. Charlotte and I met up with him as Otto complied with his request.

"Yeah. . .I'll go down to the lab personally, sir. . .Yes, we've got a substantial lead here. . .What? *Another* one? What is it this time? *Froot Loops*. Damn. . ." He made a couple of notes on the pad, then pocketed both pen and paper in his jacket.

"Lieutenant, what is it?" I heard Charlotte ask as I backtracked into the morgue. As they talked, I quickly scanned through the microfilm reels and threaded the one dated October 1991.

I had a bad feeling about this.

"I got to go," I overheard the detective say right after he hung up the phone. "Something's come up. Thanks for all. . ."

"Lieutenant," I called from the morgue's doorway. "Can I see you?"

"Not now, Blazer. I'm on my way."

"This is kind of important. Please." I tried to hide my uneasiness, but I wasn't sure it was working.

"I don't have time for this, Blazer," he said, but he walked into the morgue nonetheless. Charlotte and Otto followed. "This better be good."

"Oh, it is," I assured him.

With an unsteady hand, I directed his attention to the headline on the microfilm viewer's screen.

"TRIAL BEGINS IN RESTAURANT MURDER CASE," the simple headline read. What followed was the first in a series of articles that ran the course of my time back then when I was quite literally defending my life. A small picture of me in jail-issued coveralls ran at the bottom, alongside a snapshot of Detective Hunter Whitloe himself, with a caption that read, "We've got this Blazer fellow dead to rights."

"Did I hear you say your captain received a box of Froot Loops?" I asked, having pieced it all together. I was, after all, a "fruit."

Whitloe brushed past me and peered into the screen. Ignoring my question, he asked, "What's the by-line?"

"Guess," I said.

In a moment, he knew what I did. That the article on my trial had been penned by the infamous Garrison Fitzgerald, and that I, in all probability, was next.

"You're coming with me," Whitloe said, and I shadowed him out the door.

"Everything we've got points to this Fitzgerald fellow," Whitloe explained to Captain Colm Atherton. I stood beside the detective with all the printouts we'd collected at the *Times*, ready if he wanted to see them.

He did, and about half an hour later, he had come to the same conclusion Whitloe and I had reached when we added that piece about my trial. As we finished, Deputy Briggs came in to announce that a call to the mental facility in Napa confirmed that Garrison Fitzgerald had checked himself out about three weeks ago, just before this whole thing had started.

"Well," Atherton said, "for the first time, we seem to be on top of things. Don't worry, Mr. Blazer. We'll see to it that nothing happens to you. As of this minute, you've got round-the-clock police protection. Isn't that right, Hunter?"

"Sir?" Whitloe replied.

"I want you to handle this personally, Lieutenant. You aren't to let this man out of your sight until this Fitzgerald person is apprehended and we make it past Tuesday."

"Tuesday?" I asked. The thought of Whitloe around for the next four days made the word sound like "forever."

"If our man follows his pattern," Atherton explained, "he'll try to strike on Tuesday. Isn't that right, Hunter?"

"But sir," the detective tried. I guessed he was a little less excited with this arrangement than I was, if that were at all possible. "Don't you think that. . .?"

"What's the problem, Detective? You were jumping at the chance to watch that Kellogg boy last week, weren't you?"

"Yes sir, but Mr. Blazer and I have some fundamental differences of opinion," Whitloe said. "And I think. . ."

"You're going to follow this one through, Hunter. I don't care what it takes. And that's an order." The captain turned his gaze to me, trying to smooth over Whitloe's outburst with a gentle look. "I don't know," he suggested, "have him stay at your house. I'm sure Gladys wouldn't mind. Now, follow him over to his place so he can get a few of his things."

"Yes sir," Whitloe said.

"You have nothing to worry about, Mr. Blazer," Atherton said as we started out the door. "You're in good hands."

Walking through the police station, Whitloe mumbled to me, "That's just a figure of speech, Blazer. I don't want you getting any funny ideas while I'm around."

The man's homophobia had him so paranoid that I almost found it comical. I caught myself chiming back with, "Not to worry, Whitloe. That's *your* fantasy. Not mine."

He didn't find that amusing at all.

Chapter Ten

Snap, Crackle, Pop

"ARE YOU SURE THIS is really necessary?"

I stood beside Whitloe at the front door to my apartment, fishing for the key that would unlock the deadbolt. The idea of sharing my life with this man, even if only for the next four days, had soured a lot on the ride over here from the police station.

I'd grown accustomed to being around friends and co-workers who had no problem with my being gay, and although I never really came across as overtly flamboyant or stereotypic, I enjoyed not having to actively hide anything about me or worrying that I'd somehow slip and do or say something that would let the biggest truth in my life be known.

I didn't believe in putting up fronts. I didn't believe in lying. You wouldn't catch me taking down my gay rights march poster from the 1987 March on Washington or hiding my rainbow flag whenever a non-gay person came over to visit — an act that Ruby Slippers had once termed "*straight*ening up the apartment."

I had one closet, and I put *clothes* in it.

Serial killer or no, I wasn't giving up the small personal freedoms I'd won over the years for anyone, especially Detective Hunter Whitloe.

"Do you want to live?" came his reply. "Now, make this quick, will you?"

After I had collected my toiletries and half a week's worth of clothes in a duffel, I was ready to leave. Then I walked by Dante's food bowl and stopped cold.

"Dante. Damn."

"What is it now?" Whitloe said, standing outside.

"My dog. He's been at the vet's and I was supposed to pick him up today. I guess in all the excitement, I forgot."

The detective frowned. "I'm not letting you have a dog at my place, Blazer. I have to draw the line somewhere."

Thinking for a moment, I picked up the phone, punching in the vet's number. "I'll be in to get him tomorrow," I said after identifying myself. "Around twelve. I'll pay for the extra day in cash." Whitloe shot me a look as I hung up. "Look. This Fitzgerald guy gets his victims in the morning, right? I should be okay by myself in the afternoons. And you said he's supposed to strike again on Tuesday anyway." I brought the phone up again. "One more minute," I said, dialing again. It rang half a dozen times before. . .

"Hello?"

"Pamela. It's Paul. Are you busy tomorrow, say ten-thirty?"

"I've got nothing planned," she said. "What's up?"

"I owe you one, right? How about a little payback? Don't ask me what it is. Let it be a surprise, okay?"

Pamela Lawson giggled a bit. "My curiosity's piqued, Mystery Man. You're on."

"Great. See you tomorrow."

After the call, I closed the apartment door and locked it. Whitloe said nothing, leaving me to wonder as I followed him to his house just how I was going to convince Pamela that watching my dog for the next few days was a favor I was doing *her.*

My introductions to Whitloe's wife, Gladys, were polite and brief. After showing me the extra room where I was going to stay, she asked me if I had dinner yet.

"No," I said, "But I'm not really hungry. I think I'll just. . ."

"Nonsense," she interrupted me. "I've got a nice stroganoff on the stove, and you're more than welcome to join us."

A glance toward Hunter told me the invitation was more-or-less one-sided, but I accepted anyway. I spent a quiet meal at the Whitloe's dinner table, alternating mouthfuls of Gladys's beef and noodle concoction with little stories about my time on the newspaper or quips about my family back east. I found the detective's wife not only to be a most gracious hostess and cook, but a thoughtful, kind audience as well.

Whitloe had taken his plate out on the back patio and ate alone.

Later, as I helped clean the dishes, I looked out a window and saw him cleaning his gun.

Around ten, I retreated to my room to start work on the article I'd publish after all of this was over. I had pulled out my notes from the five strange murders and readied a pen to note paper before I got up to be sure the bedroom window was locked. When I came back, I found myself running head-first into writer's block, and about two hours later, I gave up.

Going to sleep wasn't much easier, for I was alone with my nervousness and fear, as well as the sound of conversation that came from Whitloe's room. Later, I could hear him get up and lumber around, apparently unable to drift off either.

"Look what I got," Pamela Lawson said when I went by her place the next morning. She held out a black and gray, flashlight-shaped object with two metal prongs jutting out of its end. With the flick of a switch, a blue arc of energy coursed between them, quivering like a flash of lightning.

"What, may I ask, is that?"

"It's a hand-held 'Volt Revolt,' silly," she said. "An electric stun gun. I saw it advertised on TV on one of those infomercials."

Unwilling to touch it, I kept the conversation as esoteric as possible, saying, "How much was it?"

"That's the beauty of it," she beamed. "Only five easy payments of. . ."

"Wait. Don't tell me. I don't want to know."

Just then, her Siamese cat, Nero, jumped from the floor to a nearby dresser.

"Get back, you heathen," she said to him with a turn of the Volt Revolt his way. "Remember last time?" When the cat bolted to safety, she confided, "Well, I had to try it on *something*, and it has kept him off the furniture for the most part." Reading my look as I followed the cat, she said, "Don't worry. I used the lowest setting. He was only out for a few minutes. Now, what's this payback you promised me?"

A stun gun, pepper spray classes, those karate lessons she took a couple of years back, I thought. Hell, maybe I should get her a subscription to *Soldier and Warrior* magazine or something. Then I relaxed a little, more comfortable with the decision I had made yesterday when I spoke to her over the phone.

"Pamela," I said at last, "do you know how to shoot a gun?"

***

Hunter Whitloe spent his morning at the Criminalistics Lab in Martinez, trying to excite Sydney Pincus to his cause. But Pincus was overworked as it was, and the detective's arrival had just made him more of a pest than an ally in solving crimes.

"Sorry, Hunter," he said. "We're working as fast as we can. The stuff you've given us that we have gotten around to hasn't been that great either. I can't produce miracles. Give me something interesting, and I may be able to do more."

Whitloe scrawled his name on a few evidence tags. He'd asked the criminologist for some of the items they'd brought in over the last two weeks, hoping that when laid out together, *he'd* see something. So far, that idea, too, had been a bust. He slammed down the pen in disgust when he was done.

"Sorry I don't have all the answers you want, Detective."

Whitloe exhaled, "It's not all your fault, Syd. There's a lot more to it. The Captain's got Briggs running down the hotels in the area looking for our prime suspect. Someone else is watching the guy's vacant house. And I'm the one stuck having to baby-sit some faggot who's supposed to be next. He's living under my roof, for chrissakes."

"Sounds like you need a refresher in those sensitivity training classes, Hunter," Pincus offered. He picked up the completed evidence tags and Whitloe's pen, too, filing it all away.

"Don't give me that, Syd. You don't have it going on in your house like I do."

"Tell me," the criminologist said, "if you're supposed to be keeping an eye on this guy, where is he right now?"

"He's getting his dog from the vet," Whitloe said, exasperated. "Something like that. How the hell should I know?"

***

Pamela drove me to an indoor rifle range somewhere in the town of San Leandro on Davis Drive, about forty minutes down the highway. We got out after she pulled into a dirt and gravel parking lot next to a whitewashed building that appeared as the road dead-ended.

"This is it," she said, smoothing out the skirt and blouse she insisted on wearing when I asked her to take me here.

"You look like one of Charlie's Angels," I said. "Wouldn't you be more comfortable in a pair of jeans?"

She shook her head. "Some of the men here have a dim view of women to begin with. They expect us all to be pretty and helpless, so I decided to let them be half right. Watch how they treat me when we walk in."

I did, and although there were only three others inside, I witnessed them put on airs of superiority as we approached the counter. The thick one behind the desk virtually ignored her when she said, "We'd like to rent a run and a nine millimeter semi-automatic, please."

The man gruffed some response, turning to get the necessary waivers we'd complete. After producing our I.D.s and reading the range rules, he barked, "Headgear? Targets? Rounds?"

Looking over to one of the others standing under a sign that read "GUN CONTROL IS USING *BOTH* HANDS," I detected the sense of quiet amusement. He crossed his arms and seemed to scoff at us.

"The standard," Pamela said, unfazed. "A pair of headsets, four targets — two bullseyes, two silhouettes — and two boxes of bullets. A Smith and Wesson weapon will be adequate. Two sets of goggles, too."

The attendant produced what we wanted, charging us close to sixty dollars. I paid the man and picked up everything but the gun and its ammo clip, which I left to Pamela.

At the end of our run, she said, "See what I mean? They think I'm this poor defenseless girl who has no business being here. You didn't fair too badly, but you lost points with them because you're with me."

"Well, I'm not here to impress them," I replied. I set the two boxes of rounds on the small, rubber-lined table in front of us.

"Neither am I, but watch," she said, "I'll get even."

Standing back, I let her hang the first target, one of the human form silhouettes, using the clips that stuck out at each end of a rod suspended under a wire that ran the length of our range. She flipped the toggle switch on the wall, sending it by cable and pulley about twenty-five feet away. As she donned the headset and goggles, I lifted the Smith and Wesson 9mm to examine it.

"Jesus!" she jumped when I swung the barrel around to her. "Don't do that!"

I gestured to the clip, and said, "It isn't loaded, Pamela. What's the matter?"

She snatched the gun from my hand. "That's not a good habit to get yourself into," she said. "Loaded or not, you have to treat this thing like it could kill you, because it can."

I felt a rush of stupidity and embarrassment at that moment, and I said nothing for half a minute as she loaded the clip with fifteen rounds. Finally, I apologized. Then I put on my own gear.

"Just don't let it happen again," she said. "We're not here to play, and if you don't realize that, you're too dangerous." Handing me the weapon, she said, "Here. You first."

I took the gun and turned to face the target. Placing my feet a comfortable distance apart, I brought it up, taking aim.

"Use both hands," Pamela instructed. She stepped up behind me, bringing her arms around to demonstrate. "Let the hand with the gun rest in the other. It'll help you with control. Loosen up a little," she said, with a nudge of her head between my shoulder blades, which was about where she came up to me when we stood side by side.

"That's better," she said. "Now, gently squeeze the trigger. You want it to be a smooth motion, not a. . ."

BANG!

The gun kicked, and my first shot went wild. High and to the right.

"Try it again, You've got fourteen left. Finish the clip."

When I had, she toggled the target back toward us, and together we saw that I had missed every time.

"You'd be dead," she said, noting what would have been the probable outcome had the silhouette been an actual threat. Reaching into her purse, she produced her own gun, a streamlined, silver 9mm number, and popped its clip to load it. "Go ahead and reload," she said, with a brief instruction on how to eject the ammunition cartridge from the handle of my weapon.

She sent the target back down the runway, took careful aim, then fired three times.

BANG!BANG!BANG!

When she brought the paper enemy back for inspection, I could see three small holes in it: one in the heart, one in the head, and one in the crotch.

"I threw in that last one for good measure," she said, pointing to the lowest hole. Admiring her work, she smiled and said, "Clean exit."

"Damn," I said, impressed. "I'm training here with Dirty Harriet."

"You could do worse. I could get one of those apes to come over." She indicated to the men in the reception area, who were still ignoring us.

"No thanks," I said.

"Okay, then. Try again. Just remember to relax, and try to anticipate the kick."

After half an hour, we had shot through each of the four targets when my gun jammed. Pamela took a moment to dislodge the round, then she tried to fire. It jammed again.

"I'll get you another one," she said. "We need a couple more targets and more ammo anyway."

She came back with the rifle range attendant who looked more disgruntled than someone I'd care to see in a place like this.

"What do you mean it's jammed?" he said. "There's nothing wrong with this weapon."

After taking time to load the clip, the man strung up a new bullseyed target and ran it to the very end of the run, some one hundred feet away. He took aim and fired once before bringing the target back. He'd hit it dead center.

"See," he said. "Nothing wrong with it."

Pamela moved over and took his place, taking the gun from his hand. She ran the target back to the end, then squeezed nine times before it jammed once again. Flipping the toggle, the cable sent the paper back, with exactly nine little holes circling the attendant's centered one precisely.

The man, a bit humbled, took the faulty Smith and Wesson from her, saying, "I'll get you another." He lumbered off.

"And another box of rounds, too," she called after him. "I need the practice."

By the end of a good two hours, I'd trained my hand well enough to keep most of my shots on target. I wheeled in the latest bullseye to see that my last five shots had hit within the first two circles surrounding the center. The silhouette I intended to keep as a souvenir had most of the holes at mid-chest.

"You're pretty deadly there, Blazer," Pamela said as we packed up. "Maybe I should start calling you 'Rambo.'"

"I'd appreciate it if you didn't," I replied.

When we brought the rented items back to the counter, the attendant said, "You know, Miss, me and Buck run a shooters club here every Thursday. You and your friend here are more than welcome to come join us." He smiled, showing he was missing a couple of front teeth.

"Maybe," she said without commitment. "See you around, boys." On the drive home, she said, "Thanks, Paul. That was fun. But I can't wait to get home and get out of these stupid clothes. My feet are killing me, too."

"Oh," I said, remembering the dog, "could we run by Webster Street on the way?"

"Sure, but why?"

A short time later, Dante was hobbling out of the emergency veterinary clinic ahead of us, wearing a number of bandages and a large, plastic cone-shaped collar to prevent him from biting at the dressing on his leg.

"Oh, you poor baby," Pamela said. "Does he pick up HBO with that thing?" she asked me, indicating the collar. I laughed as she continued to pamper the dog with sweet talk as she let him in her car. "What you need is a lot of lovin' don't you?"

"I was hoping you would say that," I said, getting in, too.

She stopped her cooing long enough to cast me a questioning look.

"I have another favor to ask. I need you to watch him for a couple of days for me. I'm not going home for a bit."

With a gentle push, she moved Dante to the back seat where he curled up uncomfortably, fighting the cone around his neck. "Okay, Blazer. What's going on? First the rifle range, then you want me to look after your dog. Are you in some sort of trouble?" She thought for a moment. "Does this have anything to do with that Artie Kellogg incident?"

"You could say that," I said, and on the way back to her place, I decided to fill her in. She didn't say a word until after we got home.

We put the dog in a room away from her cat, then she walked me back to my Jeep. Reaching into her purse, she retrieved her gun and handed it to me.

With a slight kiss on the cheek, she said, "Here. But I hope you don't have to use it."

I smiled. "Thanks," I said. "Neither do I."

"Just where the hell have you been?" Whitloe demanded when I returned to his house after three.

"Like it actually mattered to you," I said evenly. Moving to his sofa, I sat down and turned on the TV with a remote.

"You said you were going to pick up your dog. That was over four hours ago. How long could something like that take?"

"Who are you now? My mother?" I absently surfed through the cable channels.

Storming over, he snatched the remote from my hand. "No. But I am supposed to be protecting you. You're due to be killed by Tuesday, remember?"

I laughed. "You call what you're doing 'protecting' me? You don't even know where I've been for the last few hours! I knew it was going to turn out like this. I was testing you, Whitloe. And, I must say, you failed miserably."

The detective took a seat in the chair across from me, flustered.

"I was a little surprised when you agreed to let me go to the vet's alone," I said. "When you said that was all right, I decided to see how far you were willing to go. From what I can tell, you don't give a rat's ass about protecting me, and from now on. . ."

The front door opened, and Gladys Whitloe entered, red-eyed and sniffling.

"What's the matter, hon?" Whitloe said, getting up.

Dabbing her eyes with a hanky, she replied, "I just came from Geneva Todd's memorial service. It was so heart-wrenching to see poor Clyde that way. He wanted to do something to get all of this behind him, and even though the coroner hasn't released the body yet, he decided to go through with the service. It didn't seem to help him any though." She made her way into her bedroom to get out of her black dress, and Hunter followed her.

"You aren't going to be able to get away with another stunt like the one this morning," he said to me. "From this instant forward, I'm on you like white on rice. Got it?"

As he stepped into the bedroom, I mumbled, "Yeah, right."

With my left hand, I reached to touch Pamela's gun I had tucked into the waistband of my pants.

To my surprise, Whitloe made good on his promise to shadow me, and by early Sunday evening, I was beginning to feel more than a little claustrophobic with the man watching my every move.

I had dabbled with my article until I began getting stir-crazy. Rising up from my notes I had spread over the kitchen table, I decided to try something.

How far was this guy willing to go?

And if he was being this serious about it, couldn't I have a little fun in the process?

I moved into my temporary room, changed into a comfortable pair of blue jeans and a T-shirt, then gave my car keys a good jingle as I headed toward the door.

"Just where do you think you're going?" Whitloe asked.

You're just going to have to follow me to find out, I thought. Without a reply, I was out the door. As I pulled away from the front of the house, I saw the man hopping in his car to follow.

Ten minutes later, I parked my Jeep in the lot outside The Crystal Ball, and I joined the short line of other gay men waiting to pay the evening's cover charge. Apparently the bar had come up with the idea to celebrate the end of California's water shortage, officially proclaimed over after seven years by the necessary state politicos. "Come to the END OF THE DROUGHT Party," a poster on the club's front door read. "All well drinks half-off."

This was going to be better than I had hoped, I thought, hearing more than the average commotion from inside, topped with strains of the Weather Girls singing "It's Raining Men" over the sound system. Before Whitloe managed to park his car, seven other men joined in line behind me.

"What's all this about?" the detective said, jumping line to meet up with me.

Stepping through the front door to the young woman taking the cover charge, I said to him, "I'm not going to stay all night cooped up, and this is where I choose to go." I turned to the woman and hiked a thumb Whitloe's way. "It's on him," I said, and I smiled as I caught sight of Whitloe reaching for his wallet to pay.

"Bud Light, Andy," I called to the bartender, over the loud music. "What'll you have?" I asked when the detective caught up.

"Nothing," he said. He looked around, out of sorts.

"Make that two," I said, overriding him. I paid with a ten, collected my change after leaving a generous tip, and handed Whitloe his beer. I sent the man another smile as I strode on by, saying, "This way."

I took up a spot at a nearby chest-high cocktail table, next to a few of my friends I'd seen on my way in. "Martin," I said, "Bo. . .this is Hunter. Hunter, Martin and Bo."

"Pleased to meet you," Bo said, extending a hand.

Whitloe raised his beer to his mouth and took a long, stiff drink as a reply.

"Oh, look who's here," came the voice of Ruby Slippers. Dressed in full regalia befitting such a drag queen, she came over and threw her arms around me in warm embrace. It was just the kind of spectacle I was wishing for.

"Ruby," I said, "how are you?"

"Delicious," she replied with a wicked grin. "And who's your friend?" She forced a gloved hand into Whitloe's, shaking it firmly.

"Detective Whitloe," he said, caught a bit off guard. He looked at me. "Blazer, where's the restroom?"

Ruby answered by pointing into the general direction, and he tabled his Bud Light before heading that way. As he made his way inside, I caught sight of something new above the door: a red and white electric sign like the ones found in butcher shops that read, "NOW SERVING." When the door closed, the illuminated number increased by one.

"Nice touch," I said.

"Well, you know how much action goes on in that bathroom sometimes," Ruby said. "I just suggested that we make it a little more obvious. You know, call a spade a spade."

"Hi there, handsome," Lucky Lucy said with a hand to my shoulder. "You seem to have been able to keep yourself out of trouble."

"Lucy, hello," I replied. "Not as well as I'd have liked." I gestured to a nervous Hunter Whitloe as he came out of the bathroom, with a quick glance over his shoulder behind him. "Things have gotten a little hairy, so I have him looking after me. Whitloe," I said when he returned to our table, "you know Lucy here, don't you?"

She leaned in and gave the detective a peck on the cheek. "Detective. So I guess this means that *I'm* not in danger anymore."

Ignoring the look the detective gave me, begging an explanation, I said, "You never really seemed to be, Lucy. But I'm glad we decided to play it safe anyway."

Two others showed up, and I greeted them with a nod to Whitloe at the same time. "Davin," I said, "Nolan, this is Hunter Whitloe."

"I remember you," Davin exclaimed, and Whitloe turned pale.

"I don't think so," he said quickly.

"Sure I do. From Paul's trial."

"That's right!" Ruby shouted. "I never forget a face!" She sauntered over and draped an arm around the detective's shoulders. "You remember me, don't you, love? We had such good times together."

Nolan gave me a look to which I said, "Long story. Ask Davin."

To his credit, Whitloe stayed a little longer, until Davin asked me, "He's a little old for you, isn't he, Paul?"

"Blazer," Whitloe said, finishing the beer, "I'll wait for you in the parking lot." His exit was followed by whistles and cat calls because I guess he didn't know that some guys retreated to the lot outside for a quick blow job or jack-off session. His comment sounded more like a proposition than the simple statement I'm sure he intended.

"Fine," I said, blushing all the same. "I'm not seeing him, you guys. I swear."

Later in the evening, the music died down, and Ruby walked over to a make-shift stage and picked up a microphone.

"Good evening, ladies and gentlepersons," she growled. "And welcome to our end of the drought party here at The Crystal Ball. I hope every one's having a fabulous time."

To that, a mix of cheers and applause filled the room, and the drag queen drank it in.

"Good," she said. "So am I. But let me tell you, my day didn't start off that way. No sir. You see, I walked into my kitchen this morning to have a bowl of cereal. . .oh, you know the kind. It's called 'Queerios.'" She gave a dramatic pause that was filled with a hoot or two before saying, "You just add milk and watch them eat each other."

During the laughter and clapping that followed, the drag queen sent a conspicuous wink my way. And I found myself lightening up a little, knowing that somebody could laugh at the absurdity of the situation I was in.

"Actually," she continued, "I had to settle for *that* brand when I couldn't find my favorite in the grocery store. The cereal made for angry people. It's called 'Nuttin', *Bitch*'!"

Even I had to laugh at that one.

I ordered a round for everyone when Andy came by with a tray. When he returned with the drinks, I paid him and said, "Come here." When he had stepped in close enough, I planted a firm, wet kiss on his lips. Something inside rose when I found he was kissing back.

"Well, well," Lucky Lucy said when we came up for air.

"Talk to me later," Andy said, but before I could explain why I couldn't, he had drifted into the crowd to make his rounds.

I stayed until just before last call, leaving Ruby to make my apologies to the bartender, and I tapped on Whitloe's car window to roust him before getting in my Jeep and driving back to his place.

Chapter Eleven

Cuckoo For Cocoa Puffs

MID-MONDAY MORNING, I called the *Times* office to check in with Charlotte Journigan.

"How're you fairing?" she asked in her Southern drawl.

"Fine, I guess," I replied. I had to ignore a sarcastic grumble from Whitloe as he walked into the kitchen dressed in his pajamas. "As well as can be expected. I think the detective and I are starting to get on each other's nerves." When another grunt made its way from the kitchen, I found myself smiling.

"I'll bet," Charlotte said. "How's the story coming along? We want to run it on Page One of the afternoon edition tomorrow, after this whole thing's over, you know."

"Yeah, I know. I just hope we're both here to read it," I said.

"Speaking about this all being over," she said, "have the police found Garry yet?"

"Nope," I said, relaying what Whitloe had told me this morning after he made a call to the station. "There was a report of his name showing up on an airline roster, and they sent someone down there to check it out. Aside from that, no one's seen him since he left Napa. They've got my apartment pretty well staked out, and since he's killed his victims in their own homes, with the exception of Redford Malone, they should just be able to nab him there when he shows up early tomorrow morning."

"Moving you out of there was a smart move," she said.

"Yeah, I guess." I looked up at Whitloe as he came back into the living room with an apple in his mouth and a glass of juice in his hand. He refused to look at me as he took a chair on the other side of the room. "But we'll all be glad when he's caught, and we go back to our semi-normal lives."

"You're a trooper, Blazer. I'll give you that. Well, I'll sign off now, and. . .wait. Nicholson wants to know if the two of you would like a break and would like to come over tonight for dinner."

I heard a bit of discussion on the other end of the line, and I considered the offer and made a decision without asking my bodyguard. After last night, I figured I could get away with just about anything. "Sure," I said. "Tell him we'll be over around eight. But it can't be too late an evening. We need to be back here in plenty of time to batten down the hatches at this place."

"Eight it is," she said, confirming with Otto in the background. "Take care, Paul. We'll see you tomorrow."

"Bye," I said.

"What did you just do?" Whitloe asked.

"Don't go get your panties in a twist, Whitloe," I said. "It's just dinner with Otto Nicholson, from the paper." I got up to go to the bathroom and shower.

"I don't think I like your friends, Blazer," the detective said. "If it's all the same to you, I'll just sit this one out in the car. You two have a wonderful time without me."

"Suit yourself," I said, and a moment later, I was stepping under a cool, cleansing spray.

"Paul, good to see you. Come in," Otto said when we arrived just before eight. "Where's the detective?"

"He's decided to wait for me in the car," I replied, with a gesture back to the end of the lot where Whitloe had parked.

Nicholson stepped past me, saying, "Don't be ridiculous. Detective Whitloe," he called, "come in here. I've set the table for three." He had to walk half way down the driveway before Whitloe gave in, opening his door.

Inside, we ate a pleasant meal of grilled chicken and pasta, with Otto serving us hand and foot.

"Otto," I said, "sit down for a minute. You're making me dizzy with all of your running back and forth."

"Oh, very well," he said, pulling out his chair. "Tell me, Detective. Still no word on the whereabouts of Garrison Fitzgerald?"

Whitloe swallowed a mouthful of pasta before responding. "My deputy's sitting in the lobby of the airport, following up on that lead we got. It put him on an incoming flight from Los Angeles around nine tonight but if you ask me, it's all just an elaborate trick to throw us off track. But, we'll catch him. We've got Blazer's place well covered. When he shows up tomorrow morning, we'll be waiting for him. He'll walk right into our hands."

"Well, I must say that I'm relieved you were able to figure out all of his twisted little messages," Otto said. "He was killing people at what, a rate of two a week, right?"

"Tuesdays and Fridays," I added. "In some kind of odd pattern, I guess, but don't ask me to explain the reasoning of a serial killer."

"'Tuesdays and Fridays,'" Otto repeated, thinking. "Well, there is some warped sense to that."

"What do you mean?" asked Whitloe.

"Well, maybe it's just a coincidence," Otto explained, "but Garry wrote a column that would run every Tuesday and Friday."

"That's interesting," I said. "Otto, you said you didn't know the man very well, but you had breakfast with him in the office from time to time. Tell me, did he ever give you any clue that he'd go off the deep end like this?"

Nicholson stood to clear the table when we were through. "As I told you, Paul, I only knew him professionally. In retrospect, some of the things that he's done in connection with these crimes parallel the things

I knew him to do back then. Come to think of it, you'll never guess what he ate most often when we did have breakfast together."

"Cereal," Whitloe said.

"Uh-huh," Otto confirmed. "So that explains that, too."

Just then, a call came in on Whitloe's cel phone, hanging at his hip. He stood, unclipping it, and said, "If you'll excuse me, I'll go outside to take this."

"Certainly," Otto said, with a sweep of his arm toward the front door. "Paul, could you help me with the dishes? I'm gonna run to the bathroom."

"Sure thing," I said, and I watched as both of them left the dining room on separate quests.

Drawing the water in the kitchen sink, I looked for the bottle of liquid detergent. Finding none in view, I bent over and opened the cabinet under the sink.

"Paul," came Whitloe's voice from the area of the front door, "the battery in this thing's going dead. It's breaking up. I've got to run to a pay phone at the convenience store to call back. It was Briggs at the airport with news on Fitzgerald. His plane's coming in early, and he seems to be on it."

"Good," I replied, finding myself relaxing a lot more than I had expected to. I guess I was more keyed up than I had thought. "Go ahead. I'll wait for you to come back."

"If it is him," Whitloe said, "I'm going to the airport, too. I can send a squad car over to pick you up."

"No need," I said, finally moving around the corner of the kitchen to see him. "I can stay here with Otto and get a ride back to my place later."

"Good man," the detective said, in a tone I recognized as being genuine. I watched as he went down the drive and got into his car. As he drove away, I turned to go back to the kitchen to resume my search for the dishwashing soap. Glancing at Otto's huge saltwater aquarium as I pivoted, however, I noticed something strange.

A closer look showed me that it was Picard, the scorpionfish, floating awkwardly, upside down. He was dead, his proud fins and spines now wilted and being pecked at by some of the other fish in the tank.

"Poor guy," I said, tapping lightly on the glass. "Otto," I called as I made it back into the kitchen, "you've got a fish floating in your tank." The next line came out under my breath: "And you're not going to be too happy when you see him and realize that you're out a hundred and sixty dollars."

Opening another cabinet door, I looked for anything that resembled dishwashing detergent. What I found instead made me stop stone cold.

Staring back at me were six small, single-serving sized boxes of cereal.

Wheaties. Total. Trix. Golden Grahams. Post Raisin Bran.

And Froot Loops.

Each of them had a newspaper-clipped photo of each of the corresponding murder victims.

Matthew Black. Terry Totah. Nicholas Pirelli. Geneva Graham Todd. Redford Malone.

And me.

These must have been the mates to the ones Whitloe had received in the mail at the station. Multi-packs always carried two of each type of cereal, and *these were the fucking mates.* That meant. . .

Before I could finish my thought, I felt a sharp jolt around my elbow, and my knees buckled, sending me to the floor. Everything went black before my head hit the tiles, but the last thing I remembered seeing was the twisted face of Otto Nicholson and what appeared to be his Star Trek phaser held tightly in his hand.

Chapter Twelve

Chex Mate

HUNTER WHITLOE HAD TO try seven pay phones at two different locations until he found one that hadn't been vandalized or just simply wasn't working. When he finally made contact with the airport, he had to wait another ten minutes while the operator paged his deputy to come to a white courtesy phone.

"Lieutenant?"

"Briggs," Whitloe said, "it's about fucking time. What took you so long?"

There was some sort of ruckus on the other end of the line before Briggs came back with, "Well, we've got him, Lieutenant. Fitzgerald, I mean. He's here with a sister of his who claims he's been with her in Los Angeles ever since he left Napa. We're calling a few of her friends there to see if they can back up their story. If it's true, then this guy isn't the one we're after."

No shit, the detective thought. "Get back to me when you have something, but don't let that man out of your sight until he's brought into the station and I have a chance to talk to him. Understand?"

"Got it, Lieutenant. Oh, sir?"

"What is it now?"

"I got a call from the department before you rang through to me," he said. "Apparently Sydney Pincus down at the lab has been trying to reach you, but something's wrong with your cel phone. You should give him a call, too."

"I'll do that," he said. He hung up without saying "good-bye," then stabbed in the number to the Criminalistics Lab in Martinez. "It's Whitloe, returning Pincus's call. Yeah, I'll hold."

So it's not Fitzgerald, he thought. *If it's not him, then who?*

"Hunter," came the technician's voice, "I've finally got a match on that fingerprint from your cereal box."

"Really?"

"Yeah. It came from that pen you left when you were in on Saturday."

"Pen? What pen?" The detective racked his brain for a moment, trying to recall where he might have picked up a stray pen that would have a killer's fingerprint on it.

Then he remembered.

"Shit," he said into the receiver before dropping it and racing back to Otto Nicholson's place.

***

Lips.

I felt lips.

Groggy and weak, I felt lips pressing hard against my own.

. . .mouth-to-mouth. . .being revived by mouth-to-mouth. Safe. . . Someone's here. . .I'll be okay. . .

As my brain registered the sensation in half-thoughts, another feeling came to me.

. . .in my mouth. . .a tongue. . .wait, was this a kiss?. . .Just where was I?. . .

Straining, my eyes opened and focused on a face. Nicholson's face.

. . .a kiss?. . .from Otto. . .I never suspected. . .

Then my throat forced open and I gagged as he thrust his mouthful of pre-chewed cereal into my own.

. . .cereal. . .Froot Loops. . .

With some effort, I reached for Pamela's gun at my side when it dawned on me exactly what he was doing. He was force-feeding me my final meal, just like he had all the others. As I drew the barrel upward, however, Otto easily batted it from my hand, and it skidded across the kitchen floor.

Trying to shake off this weariness, I shook my head, only to catch a glimpse of the kitchen table which had been dressed for breakfast, complete with a glass of orange juice, a cereal bowl of Froot Loops, and a side order of toast.

How long had I been out? Long enough for Otto to have done all of this, I guessed. *Maybe twenty minutes, half an hour.*

He came at me once again, holding that phaser he'd made himself, its blue electric arcs flickering at me, to render me unconscious a second time as he finished off the job. By now, though, I'd concentrated enough of my strength for a blow that sent that thing across the kitchen to join the gun.

"Feisty one, aren't you, Paul?" he said, moving to the bottle of juice on the table in front of me. In an instant, he had the jug upturned against my mouth, and I was drowning. "Say 'when,'" he said with a laugh.

Without the strength to fight back, I simply leaned my weight to one side, falling out of the kitchen chair he had managed to lift me into for this death scene. I tumbled to the floor, spewing liquid from my mouth and nose, coughing. In my fall, one of my legs caught Otto unaware, tripping him as well. We got up at about the same time, him with a bloody gash to his head he must have received when he struck a leg of the table, me with only the power to rest myself against the wall, half-sitting.

"Otto," I said, trying to reason with him. "Don't do this. Can't you see it's all wrong?" I flung an arm lazily to the puddle around me. "What's with this?"

"Orange juice," he said with a coarse laugh. "It's not just for breakfast any more."

"Otto, it's all wrong," I repeated. "This is nothing like the others. It isn't even *morning*, for God's sake. What'll you do when Whitloe comes back?"

He calmly crossed the kitchen floor and picked up his stun gun phaser. "I've already thought of that," he said. "I'll just turn this on me, and he'll find us both unconscious. But there'll be one big difference between us, Paul. You won't be alive.

"You see, I couldn't have you live to write that story. Not after all the work I've done to do it myself. I'd thought all of this through, all with the exception of you, of course. It was supposed to be me who uncovered the killer. It was supposed to be me who would claim the glory this time."

"Fitzgerald," I said weakly, beginning to understand.

"Ah, the illustrious Garrison Fitzgerald," he repeated ruefully. "He was the one to take the fall for this. I'd left enough evidence in his own home that no alibi he could come up with would shake him from suspicion. Frankly, I'm a little surprised that the police haven't come across it. That fool Whitloe didn't mention it this evening. Maybe he's not as bright as I had thought. Well," he laughed again, "he *did* need your help in solving my earlier riddles, didn't he?"

I watched as Otto paced before me, toying with me for the time being. I used this time to regain my senses, and I did whatever I could to keep him talking while I did so.

"Why?" I asked. "Why Fitzgerald?"

"Can't you see? Garry was always the one who took the prizes. Garry was the one who went on to the Pulitzer while he left me stuck writing the obituaries. Who do you think gave him the idea for the piece that got him that award? Me, that's who.

"When I heard he was getting out of the nut house to come back to the paper, I knew I had to do something. And you see, it was all falling together so perfectly. Malone was supposed to have been the last one, but when Charlotte gave you the assignment instead of me, I decided that you had to be eliminated as well. You brought this on yourself, Paul," he said, moving in for the kill.

That was when I kicked out at the chair next to me, sending it into his groin. He doubled over long enough for me to struggle past him, and limp my way into the darkened hallway. I managed to right myself and slip into the coat closet just as a banging rattled the front door.

"Nicholson, open up!" It was Hunter Whitloe.

Otto must have been distracted because my door didn't fly open as I'd expected it to. I waited, listening for anything to tell me where he was. The next sound I heard was Whitloe as he knocked the front door in.

"Nicholson?" he yelled. "Blazer, are you all right?"

I didn't want to say anything for fear Otto would find out where I was and finish me.

"Blazer? Where are. . ."

I heard a crash, the sound of a lamp breaking maybe. Then came a struggle, and in my mind's eye, I could see Otto and the detective wrestling on the living room floor.

"You little son of a. . ."

Again, the sound of something breaking.

I drew in a few deep breaths as I heard a series of thumping noises. They were coming down the hall. If I had guessed it right, they'd be in front of my door right. . .

. . .about. . .

Now!

Flinging all my weight into the door, it slammed open and into the pair. In the darkness, I could make out the glint of Whitloe's gun he had drawn as it fell from his hand to the carpeted floor beneath him.

Damn it.

The force of the blow, however, had struck Otto more squarely, sending him tumbling head first into the open door to the room on the other side.

I bent over to help the fallen detective when another hand hit me from behind. In an instant, I was on the floor, too, nearly on top of the man who had been assigned to protect me.

Now it looked like my little maneuver had gotten both of us killed.

"Otto, don't," I pleaded one last time, bringing up an arm in my defense.

Nicholson said nothing, his silence as dark and threatening as the silhouette his figure cast in the dimly lit hallway above us. As he made a final lunge toward me, I could see the glint from the end of a hypodermic syringe in his hand.

It came down.

I rolled over, flat on my back, bringing Whitloe's weapon up in front of me in an arc. With my shoulders against the carpet, I aimed into the approaching darkness and braced myself as I squeezed the trigger.

There was a flash and a kick much stronger than any I had felt with the 9mm on the shooting range. Whitloe carried a .357 Magnum, and it bucked in my hand hard enough I was sure I had just shot the ceiling. Through the ringing in my ears, I could hear the sound of cracking and falling plaster.

Shit, I missed, I thought. I had just enough time for one lousy shot, and *I missed.* The next thing I felt was the thin, sharp prick of the hypodermic as it drove into my leg.

Then came a heavy thud that told me that Nicholson had fallen to the floor beside us.

Maybe I hadn't missed after all. The bullet must have torn through him and lodged in the ceiling overhead.

Clean exit.

Pamela Lawson's words echoed quietly through my mind, and I lay there frozen for a moment, realizing that I had just killed a man.

Then, in the silence, someone moved.

But it wasn't Nicholson. It was Whitloe.

He managed to get to his feet and find a light switch. As the brightness filled the hallway, I could see him rubbing the back of his neck where the door must have struck him. He looked past me to where our attacker lay, but I couldn't bring myself to follow his gaze. I closed my eyes as the detective stepped over me to reach the other man.

"So," he said, turning the body over. "Nicholson was the joker."

"Yeah," I replied. "And DeVito was the Penguin." Nothing like a little sarcasm to cut through the thickness hanging in my head.

"Hey, yeah," Whitloe said. "Here." He pulled the needle from my calf and handed it to me. "I guess he didn't have time to use this."

I stared at the syringe, plunger up, and still filled with a milky white fluid, most likely the poison he's extracted from the dead scorpionfish in his tank. He must have dropped it when I shot him.

"Hey," the detective said, "toss me my handcuffs, will you? They're over there. You have the right to remain silent. Anything you say. . ."

"What? Are you going to arrest me?"

"They're not for you, Blazer. They're for him." Whitloe gestured to the unmoving form of Otto Nicholson. "Don't flatter yourself, Blazer," he explained. "That shot of yours was high and to the right. You barely grazed his shoulder here. He must have jerked to the side when you hit him, and he knocked his head or something on the way down."

"So, he's going to be all right?" I took in a deep breath, relieved, as I handed Whitloe the cuffs.

"He'll live," he replied. "Long enough to stand trial for multiple murder." He said nothing further as he restrained Nicholson, then he turned to me with an expression I couldn't read.

"What?" I asked, sensing that he was suddenly uncomfortable. "What is it?"

Lieutenant Detective Hunter Whitloe flustered. "Well. . ." he began. "I mean, it *was* a good shot, you know. Even though you missed. You stopped him before he. . .eh. . ."

"You're welcome," I said, understanding what he was really trying to say.

He lowered his head a bit. "I guess it's a good thing you came out of the closet when you did."

Before he had finished his sentence, we both found ourselves laughing.

Epilogue

A Honey of an "O"

LOOKING OVER MY SHOULDER at a copy of the Tuesday afternoon edition of the *Times*, Assistant News Editor Charlotte Journigan remarked, "I like the headline." It read, "HAVING BREAKFAST WITH A CEREAL KILLER," and it had been her idea.

"So do I," noted Garrison Fitzgerald. "But the piece itself is first-rate. Definitely Page One caliber. Nice job, Blazer."

"Thank you, sir," I said humbly. "I just hope that I don't have to go through something like this the next time I write a story."

Charlotte gave me a look. "'Next time?'"

"Well," I fumbled, "I thought. . ."

"Don't go jumping the gun on us, Blazer," she said. "We only have one full-time position open on staff, but it's yours if you want it."

"The obituaries," I said. "Sure. I'll take it."

"Good man," she said with a pat to my back. "Now go and see about the fax from the Twilight Zone. I swear, that old folks home cranks them out about as fast as old Nicholson did."

Getting back to my desk, I scanned my article one final time. It ran through the list of murders, from Black to Malone, along with the cereal clues that Whitloe had been getting all the while. Toxicology had confirmed that Nicholson had used a combination of scorpionfish and octopus venom, covering it up with the addition of liquid nicotine I had guessed he had strained from Charlotte's make-shift ashtray he so dutifully emptied on a daily basis. The concentration of the nicotine had been so strong and the other so exotic and rare that the lab had never considered testing for it. A quote from the tech there promised never to let that happen again.

I told of the jealousy that Otto had experienced over his rival, Garrison Fitzgerald, and I outlined the elaborate scheme he had set up to discredit the man while gleaning a little glory for himself. In a search of Otto's house, the police had found a letter that Fitzgerald had sent him, alerting him to his upcoming release from the mental facility in Napa and his pending return to the *Times*. Fitzgerald had told him he would be off to Los Angeles for a visit with family before coming back, and he had signed it, "Your friend," with a large, cursive capital letter "G."

I guess Otto had known the man better than he had led me to believe.

On a fluke, I had landed a quote from Deputy Jonathan Briggs, who deciphered the last words of the late Geneva Graham Todd.

"She had said 'My pa—,'" he explained. "At first, we thought it was her *pa*cemaker, but in hindsight, she was probably trying to say 'My paperboy.'" I then told how Otto must have gained entrance into his victim's homes by dressing as a newscarrier, driving around in his loaned *Times* van. He hid his modified stun gun and a hypodermic he had for his diabetes — now filled with poison — in a shoulder bag usually worn to carry copies of the paper while on rounds. When he'd persuade them to let him inside to use the phone or something, he'd hit them with the phaser when they weren't looking. That gave him plenty of time to set up his trademarked breakfast scene, inject them under the tongue where it would be least detected, then force the cereal down their throats.

Graham hadn't been poisoned because the stun gun had stopped her pacemaker. Nicholson barely got away before the police had arrived, so she was spared the final meal.

I guess by the time Otto got around to me, he was a little more than frazzled. He was willing to dump his early morning and cereal M.O. for his evening attempt with the orange juice just to see me dead. When things began closing in around him, he panicked, and lucky for me he tried to move the syringe step to later in his plan.

On top of it all, Whitloe had told me he was getting calls from the cereal manufacturers General Mills, Post, and Kellogg's, wanting to file some sort of suit against Nicholson for trademark infringement and defamation.

In all, I thought it had been a decent attempt. My article, that is. I carefully folded my copy and stored it in my desk. Maybe I'd get it framed later on.

"Blazer," called Kent Abernathy. "You've got a call. Line two."

"Thanks," I said, punching the appropriate button. "Paul Blazer. Obituaries."

"Paul, it's Pamela. I just saw the front page of the *Times*. It's wonderful!"

"And thanks to you, I was able to get up this morning to write it."

She gave a small laugh. "It was nothing. Let me know when you want to go back to the rifle range, okay?"

"Sure."

"Now what other news do you have for me?"

"Pardon?" I asked.

"Today's March 9th," she said.

"And. . ."

"Don't you get your HIV results today?"

Whatever high I was riding collapsed beneath me as she spoke those words. Glancing at my watch, I saw that if I hurried, I could make it to the clinic before they closed. "I haven't gone yet. I've been busy."

"Well, get a move on, mister. Then call me with the good news."

I fidgeted a minute, wondering how I could — in all good conscience — not go and pick up my results. Losing that battle, I said, "Let me go, then. I'll call you later. How's that?"

"I've heard that before," she said. "Hey, wait a minute. You have to see me when you come by to pick up your dog. Do you know that I've caught him nosing around Nero's litter box? I think he's *eating* the cat turds."

"Almond rocha," I said, getting a visual.

"You're disgusting. I'll see you later."

"Bye."

I walked into the HIV clinic in Walnut Creek, and sat down with a counselor I hadn't seen before.

"Now, tell us again," he said, "why did you come in to get tested?"

"Look," I said, thinking, *In the past two weeks, I've had my ass reamed by my boss, my dog's been hit by a car, my ex-lover has been diagnosed with AIDS, I was stalked and nearly murdered by a serial killer who turned out to be someone I considered a friend, and I haven't gotten laid since I don't know when. Just give the fucking results, will you?* "I know that these questions must be part of your job," I managed instead, "but these last couple of days have been rather difficult. I'd appreciate it if you'd just. . ."

"Non-reactive," he said, looking at his file.

"'Non-reactive'? You mean 'negative'?"

"We don't use the term 'negative' any longer sir. We say it's 'non-reactive.'" He looked at me, waiting to see if I had any questions for him.

I didn't.

The only question I had was one for myself.

Why didn't I feel relieved?

After picking up Dante from Pamela's, I drove home to my apartment and took the mail from my tiny box near the front door. I stopped in mid-motion, however, when what I pulled out was a small, promotional-size box of Wheaties, with a dotted silhouette on the face of it that asked me to "Picture Yourself On a Wheaties Box." The accompanying card assured me that this package was legit, not another twisted message from one Otto Nicholson.

"No, thank you," I said to the box as I let the dog inside ahead of me. I almost threw the thing away, until I thought of a certain police detective who might appreciate it more than I had.

***

Hunter Whitloe slipped into his pajama bottoms and climbed into bed alongside his wife, ready for a good night's sleep. When it didn't come, after an hour and a half of tossing and turning, however, he got up and paced the floor of his living room.

He looked at the clock.

11:24.

After half a minute more, he threw aside any argument that was raging in his head and picked up the telephone.

212/696-, he dialed, then he finished with the last four digits, and fought hard not to hang up as it rang.

"Hello," came a groggy voice on the other end.

"Clayton?" Whitloe asked. "It's me, Hunter."

"Sorry, Hunter. This is David."

Whitloe paused. "You're Clayton's. . .uh. . .partner," he said at last, having to search for the right word.

"That's right," David said. "Just a minute. I'll wake him."

By the time Hunter's brother had made it to the phone, the detective started crying. He fought back years of anger, sorrow, and pain but somehow managed to stay on the line, and they talked for a good two hours. When he hung up, Whitloe made it back to his bed in the dark, and he drifted into a sleep more peaceful than he had had in years.

***

I decided to go out and have a drink at The Crystal Ball before bedding down for the night, but the place was pretty dead. I finished off the last of my Bud Light when I heard someone say, "Hey, nice shirt."

I had decided to go out wearing an aqua-colored number that read, "MY NEXT HUSBAND WILL BE NORMAL." I smiled, and it broadened a little more when I looked his direction and saw that it was Andy.

"One can always hope," I said.

"Sorry you couldn't stick around on Sunday," he said. "I was hoping that I'd run into you again soon."

"Well, here I am," I said, "and if your offer's still good, I'm interested. Normal or not."

The grin that followed told me that things were beginning to look up.

"Just let me hit the rest room first," I said.

As I stood at the urinal, relieving myself, the door opened, and another good-looking older man stepped up beside me. "What are you up to?" he asked.

"No good," I replied as I zipped up. "But my dance card's full for this evening. Sorry."

"With Andy," the man said. "I know. I was talking with him when you came in, and if you're up to it, we'd both like to take you home. I'm Peter."

A fantasy fulfilled, I thought, having been a little too rule-abiding for too long in my life.

"If not, I'll understand. Some people just aren't into. . ."

I smiled and placed a hand on his back, ushering him back into the bar. "After you, my good man," I said. When we met up with Andy, I said to both of them, "I just hope that neither of you will want breakfast in the morning."

***

Six months later, as Otto Nicholson's trial began, a young artist in Marin County across the San Francisco Bay faced his drawing table and picked up one of his many colored pencils. He started work on what would be the next in a series of trading cards devoted to serial killers and mass murderers.

Card Number One would sport the face of the one-time, local obituary writer, peering back at you from the side of an ordinary cereal box.

Acknowledgements

I'd like to take this opportunity to say a very special and sincere "Thank you" to a number of people in my life who, both wittingly and not, offered their love, support, and suggestions to me and this tale as it developed:

to my sister, Pam Gamble, who served as my first line of defense when it came to keeping in character and who is the greatest critic I could ever ask for; to my brother, Ron, his wife, Jennifer, and my friend, Mike Dadigan, who helped me complicate Hunter Whitloe's life; to my parents, Jim and Polly, for the quiet words of encouragement when my life raged around me; and to my sister, Laura, and her husband, Scott Journigan, for the acceptance and inclusion that I once only dreamt about;

to Sandi Snyder, a fan of Paul Blazer's first outing in 1993, for eagerly hopping on his second ride and enduring my nagging of "What page are you on?" while doing so; to Sue Griffin, for catching most of the clues the first time around; to my friend and pool-playing partner, Gary Thompson, who helped me through the last time I managed to write myself into a corner, without a decent way out of it; and to my first literary benefactor, James Wolfe, who offered me a dollar a page as I wrote this thing, as incentive to keep me going;

to Lisa Davis, for her inexplicable fear of ear piercings and her morbid sense of humor that I instilled in "Toe Tag" Taggert, and for taking Paul on his first trip to the rifle range; to Gerri Clark and Gretchen Prest, for our lunch time jogs around the lake; and to Nancy Hughes, for Deputy Briggs's postage stamp faux pas and a couple of other stories;

to Tim Cotie, my workout partner, for getting me to the gym three or four times a week, especially when I didn't want to go;

to Kayleen Fitzgerald at Decent Exposure Press, Washington, DC, for her constant support; to Carolyn Sorbe, for helping to drag me into the computer age; to Linda Bennett, for patiently listening and editing the manuscript as I read it aloud to her over one rather long weekend; to Felix DeJesus, for his wonderful work on the cover; and to Mitch Linagen, for believing in me and being there as everything finally came together;

and finally, to three brief saints: Timothy Albro, Mari Moore, and Scott Vasconcelles, whose friendship, honesty, and time spent with me have served as the inspiration for the next one.

Until next time. . .

About The Author

In an effort to confound his resume writers, Geoffrey Gamble has kept his list of honors and accomplishments as varied and diverse as possible.

He received a Bachelor of Arts degree in Communication Studies from Virginia Polytechnic Institute and was the first in the history of the university to receive an Honors Degree in Film, Video, and Popular Culture in 1985. He continued his graduate studies in cinema production at San Francisco State University, then began his writing career with a series of short stories and screenplays with titles including *The Half-Life Players, In the Blink of an Eye, Laughter Incorporated,* and *Can Jeremy Come Out and Play?*

He has spent a few terrifying and electric moments on stage as a stand-up comic, and every December 7th, he celebrates the anniversary of his now semi-legendary attempt at poetic free verse titled "Alien Humpty Dumpties."

In recent years, he has spent much of his time as a volunteer for the STOP AIDS Project, a graphic design assistant for the now-defunct San Francisco *Sentinel* gay news-weekly, the volunteer coordinator for the San Francisco AIDS Dance-a-thon, and as a member of the Board of Directors of Frameline, producer of the San Francisco International Lesbian and Gay Film Festival.

He began work on the Rainbow Mystery Series in mid-1993 with Book Red, titled *Deadly Outing*, which to date remains unpublished. In addition to other projects, he is currently working on Book Yellow in the series, *Forlorn Hope*.

He rents out the basement of a house some 30 miles east of San Francisco, in a community not unlike Chestnut Grove, with his dog, Lardook, and the rest of his spare time is usually spent with his boyfriend, who prefers only to be referred to here as 714.

Save $2.00 on Another Helping of "Breakfast"

Use this handy form to order additional copies of
Breakfast With a Cereal Killer
at $2.00 OFF the Regular Cover Price!

Send a check or money order for **$12.95** per copy to Decent Exposure Press.
(Add $3 for Priority Shipping for the first book and $1 for each additional book. California residents include 8 1/4% sales tax.) Orders of six or more qualify for special discounts. Call 510/678-3332 for details.

Also, visit our Cereal Killer Web Site at:
http://members.aol.com/Exposethis/DecentExposure/books.html

to download fun stuff and get the latest information on upcoming books in The Rainbow Mystery Series by Geoffrey P. Gamble.

Comments, requests, and queries may also be sent via e-mail at
Exposethis@aol.com

Name ______________________________
Address ______________________________
City/State/Zip ______________________________

Copies Ordered____________________Total Enclosed____________
($2.00 OFF Opportunity Available Only through this Mail Order Offer from Decent Exposure Press)

Send to: Decent Exposure Press, P.O. Box 6612, Oakland, CA 94603